Fiction Favours the Facts
Book 3

Mark Morgan,
Cathy Morgan and
Laura Morgan

Bible
Tales
www.BibleTales.online

Published in Australia by Bible Tales Online.

www.BibleTales.online

Fiction Favours the Facts – Book 3

ISBN (Paperback) 978-1-925587-24-1
ISBN (eBook): 978-1-925587-25-8

Cover pictures by Philip Morgan.

Free Download

Paul in Snippets

A 109-page PDF novelette by Mark Morgan.

The life of Paul painted from the Acts of the Apostles.

Get your free copy of *Paul in Snippets* when you sign up for the Bible Tales mailing list. As well as the eBook, you will receive a weekly email newsletter with micro tales, informative articles and special offers.

Visit **https://www.BibleTales.online/free-pins**

To my ever-patient wife Ruth.

Introduction

This book contains 22 Bible-based micro-tales that were first published in every second issue of the weekly Bible Tales newsletter between 20 November 2018 and 13 August 2020.

Some of the stories are about Bible characters you may never have heard of, while others concentrate on an incident in the life of one of the more famous Bible characters. Each story begins by showing where in the Bible the true story comes from.

Bible Tales Online produces Bible-based fiction – the facts of the Bible rounded out with imaginative detail to help readers participate in the lives and feelings of real people. With this collection, we have for the first time, included some stories written by other authors.

I hope you enjoy all of the stories.

Acknowledgements and thanks

Particular thanks go to Ruth, my wife, who helps me find time to write and then patiently reads what I have written – and now what our daughters are writing as well. She also humours me when I spend inordinate amounts of time on research into minute details.

Cathy, my oldest daughter, who has written two of the stories: *"The God of Big Things"* and *"What I have vowed, I will pay"*. She has also tirelessly undertaken the thankless task of copy editing and proof reading each of the stories before they were published in the newsletter, and reviewed the entire manuscript. Thanks, Cathy.

Laura, my youngest daughter, has contributed *"The Tale of Tabitha"*, as she continues to develop her ever-growing writing skills in short and longer stories.

I also thank Philip, my youngest son, for drawing the two pictures of herons used on the cover.

Feedback from a few newsletter subscribers has also helped to improve the stories, so I thank them too.

A request

In all of the books we publish through Bible Tales, I have a request to make of any reader: if you find any errors; typos, spelling errors, poor grammar, unkempt use of vocabulary, or, most importantly, errors of fact where the story misrepresents the Bible, please let me know. I can't correct printed books, but electronic versions and any new printed editions can be fixed.

Mark Morgan
www.BibleTales.online
August 2020

Contents

Part One: Old Testament

One

Mother-to-be

For the true story, see Genesis 16; 17:15-21; 18:1-15; 21:1-7.

It's really rather embarrassing: I'm an old woman, yet here I am expanding like a young wife only recently wed!

My husband, Abraham, is ridiculously happy, and, I must confess, so am I. From time to time, one or other of us just starts laughing for no apparent reason, and whenever one starts, the other always follows suit. My oldest servant says we are behaving like a pair of excited newly-weds, and maybe we are. But truly, we have a very good reason to be that way.

When we were married, we naturally expected that we would have children – after all, that's what marriage is meant to give. But year after year, nothing happened, and eventually we both gave up.

Then El Shaddai, our God, told Abraham to leave our home in Ur. God would show him a new land.

Oh, leaving Ur was hard. Nevertheless, we packed up and left, along with our father and some other family members. We stopped at Haran and stayed there until Terah, our father, died, then we went south to Canaan with Lot, our nephew.

God had already promised that Abraham would become a great nation, but once we arrived in Canaan he promised even more: the land would belong to us and to our descendants.

The problem was, of course, that we didn't have any descendants. No children, no descendants. Time had been ticking away, and, realistically, it was already much too late for me to ever have a child.

By the time we had been there for about ten years, I was desperate. Now, I know that I should have just trusted God, but sometimes I don't find that as easy as I should.

Then I came up with the perfect solution – or so it seemed. True, it wouldn't quite be my child, but the mother would be my servant-girl, Hagar, and the father would be my husband. It would be the best we could do. When I think back on it now, it's rather a horrible thing for a wife to plan, but, as I said, I was desperate. It seemed a simple way to get the child that God had promised us but wasn't quite delivering. If I had just trusted God and waited, I wouldn't have had all the problems with Hagar, and we wouldn't have this boy Ishmael around. Who knows how much trouble he and his offspring will cause in the future?

Faith is always easier to justify in hindsight than it is at the time when we have to choose our path.

I spoke to Abraham and he agreed to my plan. To this day, I don't really know whether he thought it was a good idea or not, but he saw that I had my heart set on it and didn't argue. I wish he had.

So I gave Hagar her orders and made all the arrangements with Abraham. And just a few weeks later, with a look of contempt, Hagar told me that she was pregnant. It wasn't hard to read her thoughts: "He's not too old to get me pregnant, but you're not a real woman."

It hadn't occurred to me that she would feel like that and I was very upset. Upset and angry. Crying as I told Abraham, resentfully blaming him for everything.

He was too kind to argue, saying that she was my servant girl and it was up to me what I did with her. I didn't realise at the time just how generous he was being in that, either, and I probably would've been furious with him if I had realised. You see, Abraham has always been very fond of Ishmael and, looking back, I have no doubt that he would have liked to lavish great care on Hagar during her pregnancy, just as he is now doing with me. It's what he is like: generous to a fault. Instead, he left it up to me, and I mistreated her harshly.

When I think how tired I have been at times during this pregnancy and remember how I demanded incessant physical work from Hagar while she was pregnant, and even ridiculed her when her increasing size made her work awkward, I feel ashamed. But at the time I was bitterly determined to pay her back for getting pregnant – illogical though that was.

I thought I was the one who had been most cruelly mistreated – by both my husband and my slave.

After a while, my callousness drove Hagar to run away, only to return a few days later with a story of God having spoken to her, telling her to come back and submit to me.

I had very mixed feelings. I didn't really want her or her baby at all, but at the same time I was actually quite relieved that she hadn't got lost in the wilderness and died. I was forced to believe her story, and that meant God was relying on me to look after her properly! Well, I did my best, and so she ended up with a son, Ishmael, while I still had none.

My husband loved Ishmael, and that hurt too.

For 13 long years, it hurt.

Then one day God spoke to my husband and told him that I was going to have a baby in a year's time, and that we were to call him Isaac.

By then, I was 90 years old. 90! Did you ever hear anything more ridiculous than the idea that a 90-year-old woman could have a baby? Knowing that it was El Shaddai who had said it made me pause in my scoffing, but still....

Be that all as it may, there was something more important to be done immediately. God had said that all of the males in our camp had to be circumcised as an ongoing sign of the covenant he was making with Abraham and his descendants. Including Ishmael.

Abraham got on with the job immediately – that's what he's like – and for a few days all of the males in the camp were rather sore. Of course, that meant there was a lot more work for us women to do while they recovered, and that effectively took my mind off the crazy idea of me having a child.

But God didn't let me forget it. Within a week, he repeated the promise, this time through three men who seemed to just appear in front of my husband while he was dozing at the door of the tent during the hottest part of the day. All of a sudden we were all busy making a meal, and then Abraham talked with them as they ate. I was standing just inside the door of the tent – not eavesdropping, of course, but making sure that if they needed anything, I could get it immediately.

When I heard my name it grabbed my attention, and I heard exactly what he said: "I will surely return to you about this time next year, and Sarah your wife shall have a son."

To be honest, my inability to have a child has overshadowed many other things in my life. If we use our hands a lot they can be rubbed raw, but over time they grow calluses. When things hurt us emotionally, we tend to develop some form of protection in the same way. For me, it is laughing – when people talk about children, I laugh, to try to hide just how much it hurts.

So when I heard this man say that I would have a child I laughed. Just quietly – there was no way anyone could have heard it.

But, somehow, he did hear.

He must have been an angel or something sent from El Shaddai himself. My husband says that he was really speaking the words of God; that it was just the same as talking to God – which my husband has done on several occasions.

"Why did Sarah laugh?" he asked, and repeated that I would have a child at about that time next year.

His ability to hear my almost-silent laugh frightened me and I lied, saying that I had not laughed. He wouldn't let it go and repeated the statement that I had indeed laughed, and I suppose I sort of admitted it.

After a while, the men were ready to leave, and Abraham walked some way with them.

I stayed in the tent, sitting back and thinking hard.

Would I really have a child?

Was it possible?

Could I let myself hope that it was possible?

I wanted to hope, but the calluses around my heart made it hard. Giving way to hope would make it so much harder afterwards if it didn't happen, and it had been many years since having a child was even a physical possibility for me. But I knew that God kept his promises.

I sat and I struggled, and as I did so, my lord Abraham was struggling too – although I didn't know it at the time. He was trying to save the life of our nephew Lot. God told him that he was going to destroy Sodom and Gomorrah, those evil cities, and we knew that Lot and his family lived in Sodom.

Funnily enough, this incident that meant death to so many provided the certainty that allowed me to give myself over entirely to hope. The very next morning, we saw God's terrifying judgement as fire and destruction fell from heaven on Sodom and Gomorrah.

It gave me the confirmation I needed: if God could do something so great, he could easily make me have a baby. So I gave myself over to hope, and that's when things began to get exciting.

Over the next few months, I began to feel younger. People have always said that I am good-looking, but in those couple of months, I actually began to agree with them. It was amazing. As I had grown older, my skin had become thinner and less resilient, and despite what people kindly said about me, I knew that I had grown wrinkled. But suddenly it was as if time was going backwards and I was getting younger. The age spots on my hands disappeared, my skin felt better and my hair started to shine again.

Abraham noticed it immediately and we were both not-so-quietly amazed. I couldn't help holding out my hands in front of me and just looking at them. Each day they looked younger and younger. Fewer wrinkles, and no pain in my joints. Everything was delightful, particularly when it became clear that my dear husband thought so too.

In some ways, it really was like being newly married all over again. We both enjoyed it very much.

And then, at just the right time to match God's promise, I found that I was pregnant.

So now, here we are, waiting for the day when our son will be born. When I first decided to embrace hope in God's promise, I still feared what would happen to an old woman trying to give birth to a child. Could I live through it? I suppose I still don't know the answer, but I'm not worried now because physically, I'm not an old woman any more.

Abraham and I still laugh many times every day, and whenever we start, we look at each other and laugh some more. I used to laugh to mask my suffering, but God knew it all anyway. Now he has combined laughter and a baby as only El Shaddai could. At God's command, our baby will be named "Isaac" – laughter.

Two

On Dry Ground

For the true story, see Exodus 14:1-15:21.

I feel rather foolish now that it's all worked out well.

Just a few hours ago, I was terrified – sure that we were all going to be slaughtered! Now all the people who threatened us are dead and we are safe and happy.

I'm just an ordinary man. I was a slave just like everyone else. I complained about the Egyptian overseers who demanded that we make a ridiculous number of bricks. I complained even more when Moses came along and we were expected not only to make bricks, but also to find the straw for them. I complained when all the water in the Nile was changed to blood: after all, what were we supposed to drink? And the frogs that came next were disgusting. What else can I say? Walking around trying to find enough room to put my feet and still ending up stepping on slimy frogs all the time. Then, going to bed at night... I think you can imagine for yourself what it was like trying to clear a space in the dark to lie down, and waking up frequently during the night with frogs all over me. Once I woke up with one frog's foot in my mouth and another in my ear! Finally the frogs went away –

but then it was gnats. It wasn't possible to avoid getting them in my mouth. I was eating mouthfuls of gnats, and other gnats were biting me all over. It was hard to work out who was getting more food from whom.

Naturally, I complained along with everyone else. Moses wasn't helping us at all. Everything had just got worse since he appeared.

When the fourth plague came, though, there was a reprieve, because Goshen where we lived was free of the flies that filled the rest of Egypt. That got me thinking a bit, but it wasn't as if there was any clear line where there were flies on one side and none on the other. If we went anywhere outside Goshen, we slowly started to meet flies, then more and more until the air – and your mouth, hair, eyes, ears and everything else – were full of flies. It was as if there was some reason why the flies didn't like Goshen. Well, I didn't care whether it was natural or not, I was just glad that we didn't have the flies or any of the other plagues that followed. Our cattle didn't die, we weren't covered with boils, no hail fell on us, and no locusts swarmed in Goshen. For once, we were doing rather well, and I wasn't complaining then – except about the work we still had to do, of course.

The darkness was yet another plague, and we didn't have that either. We could see the sun and moon as usual – as long as we didn't go outside Goshen. If we did, they gradually got dimmer and dimmer until they disappeared completely in the tangible blackness that filled the rest of the land.

That was all very good, but if the plagues were meant to bring Pharaoh to heel, then it wasn't working. Pharaoh was still refusing to treat us any better than he had been doing. Nothing that Moses brought on the land made any difference. Oh, in the middle of a plague Pharaoh would admit that he had been a bad boy, but when the heat was off, so was his remorse. He could turn contrition on and off as it suited him.

The last plague, however, did the trick. It was overwhelmingly convincing. Beforehand, Moses warned us that firstborn sons all over the land – including Goshen – would be killed on one particular night unless we followed some fancy instructions that he gave us.

It was inconvenient all right, but we got everything organised and were quite careful in obeying those instructions – even to keeping a lamb inside for four days and then slopping its blood on the doorposts of the house. I suppose it worked: my son is still alive, whereas I hear that all of the firstborn Egyptians died that night. Quite a few Egyptians had moved in among us Hebrews by that time. Some of them seemed to want to learn about the God that Moses was talking about, while others were just trying to avoid the plagues, even to the point of being willing to live among slaves to do so. Goshen's not the most upmarket neighbourhood in Egypt, but even a slum is attractive when it is the only place free of locusts and the other plagues Moses kept bringing. And, of course, the guards and taskmasters lived in Goshen to make sure that we were kept under control.

When midnight came, a sudden hubbub of screams and wailing broke out from among our Egyptian "neighbours". Once I worked out what it was about, I was glad to hear it. So many Hebrews – babies, children and adults – have died through the brutality of the Egyptians that it seemed only fair for them to get their share of death and mourning.

Then we were leaving Egypt and the Egyptians were giving us presents! I still haven't figured that out. Ah well, it meant that we were all richer than we had ever been before and had a lot more to carry than you might have expected a bunch of slaves to own.

Leaving was hard. We didn't know where we were going and we weren't used to walking long distances. Everyone was glad to go in some ways, but it wasn't long before we started to notice the problems. Sand gets into everything. Dust fills your mouth, nose, eyes and everything. Heat and hard walking. No houses.

But I thought we were coping well enough until we had that unaccountable change in direction, back down the coast. Moses told us that it was God's instruction, and since he was the only one who knew the area at all, we had to take his word for it. Dust and sand are my strongest memories of the days after we left Goshen. I've never breathed so much dust or got so much sand in my eyes. Countless tramping feet meant endless clouds of dust. Moses told us that there was a pillar of smoke sent by God to lead us, but I was too far back in the dust to be able to see anything like that, and I'm not prone to believing things that I can't see. I have to admit that there did seem to be some light, though – sometimes it almost looked like a column of fire when we stopped for the night.

In summary, it wasn't a particularly enjoyable trip, but everything was progressing well enough and we were rather pleased to be leaving Egypt. Then one afternoon as the sun was setting and we were getting ready to camp for the night, our doom caught up with us.

Most of us had been keeping a bit of a lookout behind us. Not a constant watch, you understand, just the occasional check. We'd had enough experience of Pharaoh to be a little worried that he might chase us. By that time, though, we'd begun to hope that we'd got clean away. It was not to be. As the sun sank in the west, people began to notice small clouds of dust on the horizon – clouds that grew larger as we watched.

Everybody stopped setting up camp and stood, staring in fear at those clouds of dust. Before long, it was clear that there was an army marching after us, and who else could it be but Pharaoh?

Quite understandably, I think, we panicked. I don't mean that we dropped our goods and started running away, but many people did start calling out, asking for God to help us. Others of us formed a delegation and went to remind Moses that we had told him while we were in Egypt that he should leave well enough alone – being a slave wasn't great, but it was better than being dead! At that stage, it looked as if we were all going to die in the desert, and there was a lot of worry and anger directed at Moses.

Moses told us not to worry, but really, what else was he going to say? Seriously, it didn't sound very convincing to me. Anyway, while we were talking to Moses, arguing against his glib "Just wait!" message, there was some thunder that almost sounded like a voice. Some people even said that God was telling Moses what to do, but most of us didn't hear it that way. Just thunder, I reckon.

Nevertheless, Moses had an idea, and he made his way to the beach and waved his staff around over the water.

By that time, it was almost completely dark, and that sort of cloud that Moses makes so much of moved from between us and the sea to being between us and the Egyptians. A flimsy sort of cloud wasn't going to do much to keep the Egyptians away, I thought.

But for some reason, the Egyptians didn't come and attack us straight away – definitely some bad leadership decisions there.

On the other hand, we were very fortunate with the weather, too. A strong east wind sprang up right when we needed it and there was so much dust and sand blowing around that I suspect it took the Egyptians a long time to find exactly where we were; long enough that, by the time they did, it was too late.

Anyway, after that peal of thunder, Moses told us all to move forward – straight towards the sea, mind you! By that time, it was pitch dark: the moon still hadn't risen and the stars were no help, with all the dust and sand in the air. I suppose that there was a little light from that cloud, but it didn't help much either.

Still, some of the leaders started to follow Moses' instructions straight away, marching happily off into the darkness. Crazy!

I didn't know what was the best thing to do. Nothing seemed to be able to convince Moses that he should try some other plan. After all, it was just a matter of time before the Egyptians would be in amongst us, killing and maiming, and walking out into the water wasn't going to help, was it?

It took me a long time to get back to where my family was – there weren't many landmarks to work from and there were panicking people everywhere.

The wind was blowing harder and harder from the east, and by that time men sent by Moses were spreading through the people, telling them to move forward towards the beach because we were going to walk through the sea on dry ground! There were also conflicting rumours flying through the crowd, some suggesting that people were walking across the top of the water and others saying that the leaders had disappeared into the water and no-one knew what had happened to them. Others talked about tunnels opening up in the water, while still others reported that things were happening just as Moses had said they would. It all sounded very contradictory, and about as likely as the idea that Pharaoh had followed us so that he could wish us a happy journey!

As I thought about the whole unlikely plan, I knew that I didn't want to walk on water, or in dripping tunnels through the water. Imagine having to worry about whether my wife and children had started to sink in the dark or whether the tunnel might have collapsed somewhere in front of or behind us. No, if I had to somehow walk across the Red Sea, I wanted the water to open up and make a wall for us on either side, a canyon opened through the water – but, of course, nobody could do that!

But I was still worried about the Egyptians. What if they found us because of the light that came from that pillar of cloud or smoke? Conversely, how could we see where to go in the dark of the desert night?

It seemed to me that keeping away from the Egyptians was the first thing to concentrate on, so I was eager to obey when finally we were told that it was our turn to move forward towards the beach.

I don't know how the Egyptians failed to find us all through that long night, but I wonder if the wind helped to keep us safe. After all, I wouldn't want to search in the darkness while a strong wind hurled sand in my face, if I knew that all I had to do was wait until morning and then I would be easily able to find the crowd I was looking for, trapped against the sea.

But I was glad to get moving, despite having no idea where the people who were in front of us had gone – maybe they had walked into the water and drowned, or maybe everyone had miraculously learned how to swim. Certainly Moses has managed some amazing things in the last few months, I have to admit that.

Slowly we made our way down to the beach, and then, at last, the faint light from that pillar showed what was happening: the water had opened up. It was like looking along a canyon where the walls were made of water. And down into the canyon were marching all the people of Israel, our entire nation. There were people of all ages, young and old, many leading or driving sheep and goats or cattle. As I peered further into the gloom, I could see just how far in front the line of people stretched – down, down, down, far below the level of the water. It was an incredible sight: completely unbelievable. I could even see some carts down there, pulled by slow-moving oxen. My life over the last few months has been full of strange experiences, but this was the strangest of them all. It was just light enough to see, but still dark enough to make it all seem as if it might be a dream. A dimly visible column of people stretched far ahead of us into the middle of the Red Sea, with walls of water towering above them on either side, but none of it touching any of them.

We joined the masses of people pouring down into the canyon like dust through a funnel. As we hurried across the beach, we had to squash up together a bit, but, even so, the column entering that impossible chasm must have been about 1,000 people wide. Once across the beach, we followed the contours of the sea-bottom down below the water level. I'm quite tall, and it was strange to look over the heads of the crowd towards the dark walls of water and see them gradually growing higher and higher as the "road" sank lower and lower.

You may think me peculiar, but as the wall of water on our left grew taller and taller, I was tempted to fight my way over to it and *touch* it! What did it feel like? Was it hard like ice, or what? Regrettably, a feeling of responsibility kept me near my family, so I never got the chance to find out, but I did see some goats walking next to it and it was as if they were walking beside a wall on one of the streets in Goshen. They seemed to be able to push against it without it giving way at all, and certainly without it springing a leak! On the other hand, I also saw many parents very carefully keeping their children away from the walls. I think I can understand why – who would want to be the one whose child broke the spell and drowned everyone? But for myself, I found that I was beginning to have a bit of faith in Moses, and maybe even in Yahweh. I have tried in this narrative to describe how I really felt at the time, and by this time in the night I was, for the first time in my life, genuinely starting to feel some confidence in a power that I could not see or touch. I still couldn't understand why this power – let's call it "Yahweh", since that's what Moses uses – would want to look after us at all, but he genuinely seems to want to do so. And given that he seems to be consistently able to do the sorts of things we need, it didn't seem to me worthwhile getting worried about things any more. That's faith, I suppose. My grandfather used to talk to me about faith and trust, but I could never really accept any of it, until now! Now I really see it working. And now that I see it, I feel able to extend it to a confidence that is not based on anything other than a confidence that Yahweh will be *consistent*, and that he isn't capable of making the sorts of silly little mistakes that might leave us all drowning because a little child poked his finger into a wall of water! It just wouldn't make sense.

The waning moon had risen by that time and we hurried on in the gloom, glad that we could see as much as we could, but wishing there was more light and less of a howling gale blowing in our faces. The walls of water towered over us by that time and most the people near us were moving as quickly as they could. When people spoke, there was fear in their voices, but mostly people were silent and their faces were grim. Strangely enough, I felt differently. I was gradually noticing more and more things that were utterly amazing about this midnight march along the bottom of the sea.

I saw old people who would normally have to pick their way carefully over such a rough surface, but they were walking easily, moving like much younger people. I saw many young children walking without tiring, and many others being carried effortlessly by parents or friends. My own children were walking without complaining, and that is unusual – they get their skill in it from me.

We walked all night and the wonder of walking on the dry sea bottom began to pall for many, but we finally arrived at the other side as the dawn began to lighten the sky above. The beach was crammed full of people – it didn't seem to have occurred to anyone that they needed to clear the area to make space for the thousands of people who were still climbing up out of the dry depths.

Moses had sent men through the crowds to tell people to keep moving away from the beach, but it all took time, and so moving the entire multitude out of the water canyon that Yahweh's hand had made took longer than it should have.

I stopped right where the water's edge had been only the previous night, pushed unavailingly by the crowds behind us, as the beach was too packed with people for us to move onto. Turning around, I could see the surging column still making its way up the canyon towards me, while in the far distance the beach on the other side of the sea lay empty. As I watched, I suddenly noticed that the cloud that I had dismissed as a merely coincidental phenomenon was rapidly approaching the opposite beach, and soon was moving out over the water towards us until it caught up with the stragglers of our nation. Then it slowed down and moved at their speed.

It was a scene of exquisite beauty filled with contradictions and unheard-of circumstances. The warning glow of a coming sunrise was spreading its fingers across the sky and lighting up an impossible canyon with walls of solid water. Throngs of people were hurrying across the dry sea-bottom, where people should never be. And the cloud that had followed us from Egypt was hovering over the canyon, seeming to urge the walkers on as it glowed from within with an ethereal light.

It took my breath away and made me marvel at the power of Yahweh with all the inexpressible joy of my newfound faith.

Then came the sight that once more filled me with dread. Men began to appear on the opposite shore, scurrying about like ants, and within moments it was obvious that this was the Egyptian army I had been so afraid of last night. Soon I could see horsemen and chariots, as well as the cream of Pharaoh's fighting men, gathered on the beach.

It was all very well to have an open path through the sea that allowed *us* to escape, but if we could travel through it, so could the Egyptians!

℘

And sure enough, that's what Pharaoh's army did. The foot soldiers stayed on the distant beach, but the chariots and horsemen raced down between the walls of water toward us.

So much for faith and confidence! My certainty of Yahweh's power and his care for us dissolved as I watched. I put my hand to my mouth in shock and watched as Pharaoh's army poured down into the canyon that we had traversed so slowly during the night. The dry sea-bottom would be as good a road for them as it had been for us, and it was obvious that our fate would be every bit as bad as the worst we had imagined the night before.

Full of despair and anger, I watched the inevitable unfolding before me. My anger was directed against Moses and God because it seemed that they had led us into a disaster that was even worse than our initial problem of slavery. Even slaves can die at a good old age, but Pharaoh wasn't likely to let us off easily when his land had been ruined by plagues – plagues that had culminated in the death of his own oldest son, and millions of others besides.

No, as I watched the chariots speeding easily towards me, I was sure that soon I and my wife and children would all be dead.

But there was still that pillar of fire and cloud between us and them. It not only filled the width of the canyon, but also towered above the water of the sea. Its roiling mass was close behind our rearguard, which by now was making its way up to the beach.

In earlier making sure that we were clear of the beach and out of the way, we had ended up off to one side of the canyon, and so I could see past the pillar. The light it shed was bright enough to show even the far side of the Red Sea as the light of the coming day slowly grew around us.

By that time, all of Pharaoh's chariots and mounted men were down inside the Red Sea Canyon and charging towards us, the chariots in the lead, the rumble of their wheels and the thundering of the horses' hoofs filling the early morning air. The ones in front had passed the lowest point and were climbing up toward us, the horses straining in their harnesses, seeming as eager as their masters to reach the shore where the quarry waited.

Yet the pillar of fire and cloud was still in their way. Would it be hot enough or frightening enough to stop them somehow?

I've got to tell you that it wasn't a short distance across the sea at that point! We had been walking for much of the night to cross it, and as the chariots galloped across, effortlessly swallowing up the distance we had struggled so hard to cover, the last of the people of Israel finally made their way out of the water-walled canyon and up onto the beach. By then, my family had moved away from the beach area and, with others, were climbing the slopes towards a range of mountains that lay before us. As I surveyed the rugged terrain, I thought that maybe it would be possible to hide amongst the scattered boulders or in the ravines that led towards the foothills, and thus make our way into the mountains and safety.

But Moses had said that Yahweh would fight for us, and at that moment I realised that I had to decide whether I believed what he said, or what my eyes were telling me. Could I believe in something that I had no proof of, or would I accept the obvious?

I decided to stop and watch what was happening. I wasn't completely sure, but I had a sneaking feeling that Moses might be right. I wasn't so sure about Yahweh at that moment, but I did have a little hope and confidence in Moses.

And as I watched, something changed. The leading chariots had almost reached the column of fire, but now they seemed be struggling. The horses' free-flowing gallop seemed to suddenly become hard labour. Some of the chariots didn't seem to be able to travel in a straight line any more, and I'm sure that I saw wheels falling off several.

Soon the column of chariots that had been spread out along the floor of the Red Sea began bunching up as the ones behind tried to slow down to dodge the ones in front that had suddenly lost speed. By that time they were close enough that

I could see many of the men in the chariots jumping down to try to do something to the wheels of their chariots or the harnesses of their horses. At first they seemed to have a matter-of-fact "something's wrong, I need to fix it" attitude, but after a while it became clear that the progress of the column had stopped completely. There was lots of desperate movement, but no progress as they jostled together down there in the canyon. A clear road lay before them, but maybe they could see some problems down in the sand that I couldn't see from my vantage point. I had walked across the same place without any difficulty, but maybe collecting all that water into massive walls began to cause problems after so many hours. Maybe, I thought, the water was seeping through under the sand. And I guess that that's what Pharaoh and his men were thinking too.

"Stand still," Moses had said, and I decided to obey. Due to the slope of the land at that point, the entire multitude of Israel was in a position where we could either watch Pharaoh's army gradually giving way to doubt and fear, or scurry away like rats, looking for a place to hide.

In that frenzied moment, I saw my doubts and my available choices with a strange clarity. I had to choose whether to give way to fear, or to have confidence in something I could not control. The difficulty was that many of the people behind us wanted us to keep moving and would not respond to my encouragement to turn around and watch what was unfolding behind them. Nevertheless, some of those in front were standing in our way – immovable – with their eyes fixed on the Red Sea, the water of which seemed to be moving somehow. When I almost gave in to the insistence of the people behind me to keep moving forward, those people in front were the perfect excuse: I couldn't move forward – they were in the way!

So I stood and watched, gradually noticing that more and more people were stopping and watching. Standing expectantly. Standing, I suddenly realised, in silence. The howling wind that had been blowing into our faces all through the night had slowed and stopped.

Back in the canyon, Pharaoh's chariots and horsemen were having a hard time of it. They had expected an easy victory, but everything seemed to have gone wrong for them as they approached the pillar. Their wheels were stuck in the surface that had seemed so dry when they had started galloping across, and with the cessation of the strong wind, the walls of water that towered high above them seemed to be starting to waver and wobble.

Fear spread through their ranks, and the leading chariot tried to turn around, maybe in hope of hurrying back toward the far shore. Yet the problems that had brought them to a standstill didn't seem to have gone away. As the driver struggled to whip the horses into motion, they appeared to be floundering as if in deep mud, and then one of the wheels of the chariot fell off. Quickly, the men in the chariot leapt out and began desperately to run away from the pillar, away from us, away from everything they now feared. But the thing that they really needed to fear was already thundering towards them along the canyon. The walls of water near the other side of the Red Sea had burst and a maelstrom of foaming water was rushing down towards the lowest part of the sea bottom. It engulfed horses and horsemen, picking them up like so many leaves and throwing them around in the flood; then finally flinging them into the sea, where the remaining walls of water were dissolving. Chariots and horses were hurled against those weakening walls and immediately disappeared into the depths of the sea. At that precise moment, the first rays of the rising sun threw their golden light on the scene. The light shone and sparkled on the water as the walls collapsed inward and massive waves crashed down on Pharaoh's men. Sunlight from behind us and fire from in front threw the light of Yahweh on the utter destruction of Pharaoh's army, and all of the multitude's gasps changed suddenly to cheers of joy.

Yahweh's canyon of salvation was gone, its purpose achieved. The restoration of the surface of the sea had then punished Egypt for generations of cruelty to my people.

Later, I heard that Moses had originally lifted his staff to open the path through the water, and just before that astonishing moment of sunrise, he had lifted his staff again to close it.

I have never felt such joy and confidence, yet it was mixed with some fear as well. Only a couple of hours before we had been walking down there, on a path that was now far below the water. My family – my wife and my children – had all been there. What if the water had collapsed while we had been there? God had looked after us alright, but what raw power! And I couldn't help wondering what might have happened if we had somehow angered him while we were down there. A feeling of awe filled me because of the astonishing power that Yahweh had shown – but it was a power over which I had no control at all. Would that power be there to help us the next time we needed it? I consoled myself with the knowledge that at least Moses was there to talk to God for us.

That was an amazing morning. Moses had a song to teach us and, after some practice, it was a glorious experience singing with so many, many triumphant voices spread out across that vast area. As we sang and rejoiced, many bodies of dead Egyptians washed up on the shore – mute testimony to the truth of the words of our song:

"I will sing to the Lord, for he has triumphed gloriously;
the horse and his rider he has thrown into the sea.
The Lord is my strength and my song,
and he has become my salvation;
this is my God, and I will praise him,
my father's God, and I will exalt him.
The Lord is a man of war;
the Lord is his name."

Moses' sister, Miriam, also led the women in singing and dancing. Even my wife went and joined in, although she is not normally an enthusiastic singer. That was beautiful too.

It was a delightful morning and I have never known such happiness or thankfulness. God truly has saved us!

Since then, we have stayed near the sea resting. We walked all through the night to cross the sea and everyone is tired.

Tomorrow, we will start our real journey towards the Promised Land, returning at last to the place where Abraham, Isaac and Jacob all lived.

What an exciting journey that will be – the perfect opportunity for all of us to learn how to walk with God!

Three

I was Just Thinking...

For the true story, see Numbers 26:33; 27:1-11; 36:1-12; Joshua 17:1-10.

"I was just thinking," said Mahlah, meditatively.

Noah, Hoglah, Milcah and Tirzah all looked at each other, raising their eyebrows and shaking their heads slightly. "Oh no!" they chorused in unison.

It looked almost like a practised routine as their gazes returned to the original speaker.

Over the years, the sisters had had frequent experience with Mahlah's thoughts. They normally led to trouble or inconvenience for everyone.

Even back when Mother and Father were still alive, Mahlah's "I was just thinking" statements had been somewhat of a family tradition.

Five daughters had been God's blessings for Zelophehad, and he would not have been without any one of them. However, he would have appreciated a son to round out the family – but it was not to be.

Mahlah was the second of his crop of daughters, and a thoughtful lass she was. Those words fell naturally from her lips, always accompanied by a pensive, reflective, contemplative expression, and a gaze that seemed to stare through her audience as if they weren't there.

Mother had tried to discourage Mahlah from thinking too much. Girls, so mother said, should leave excessive amounts of thinking until after they were married. There was time enough for thoughts once a husband had been safely procured. The knitted brows of a pensive look detracted from a girl's beauty, she said – and, anyway (although at only seven years of age Mahlah didn't need to worry about it quite yet) she would find that men didn't like women who thought too much.

Mahlah tried to oblige Mother, but she simply couldn't help herself. Juggling ideas and thoughts, examining the possibilities and opportunities of life – these things were as natural to her as was barking to a dog or flight to a dove. And she always seemed to foresee the tricky, complicated situations that nobody else had imagined.

If Mother had lived to see how Mahlah's persistent thinking was to make her daughters famous, she might well have died of embarrassment!

There were many other families among the Israelites that had daughters but no sons. But none of the other families had Mahlah, so it was Zelophehad's daughters who became the classic case study for exceptions in inheritance law for the whole nation.

Yet, even so, it is unlikely that Mahlah's incessant thinking would have brought them quite so much fame without Noah, the oldest daughter. It was Noah whose determination forced the world to acknowledge her sister's thoughts, and her father's heritage. She had been named after the greatest boat-builder the world had ever known, a man whose righteousness and determination are universally admired – so much so that few use the name for their sons lest they be overwhelmed by the load of expectation that goes with the name. Zelophehad, however, had not been afraid of that load and had even been willing to apply the name to a girl-child. Of course, he expected to have a son later as well, but, nevertheless, he had high hopes for this, his first daughter.

But the question always in the background was whether he would see her grow to adulthood.

It was a strange time in the history of the nation – in fact, in the history of the world. Every adult in the nation was facing a deadline and they knew it, and many were dying even earlier in sudden plagues.

Years earlier, everyone in the twelve tribes of Israel who was 20 years old or over had been condemned to die in the wilderness after they had refused to obey God's command to enter the Promised Land and conquer it. Zelophehad had been a young man then, just 22 years old,[1] and he had listened with the rest to the brave heroes who had spied out the land over 40 days and brought back such a terrifying report. It wasn't that the land wasn't wonderful in many ways, they admitted – it was just that its idyllic characteristics had spawned the biggest and strongest defenders that could be imagined. In fact, the giant warriors reported by the spies were even bigger than could be properly imagined – big enough to terrify both the witnesses and their hearers.

---

[1] We do not know Zelophehad's age at any stage, except that he was 20 or over when the Moses sent spies into the Promised Land.

It was true that two of the spies, Joshua and Caleb, while acknowledging the apparent difficulties, had claimed that Israel would have no trouble taking over the land with God's help. But that had sounded fanciful, and young Zelophehad had been no more convinced than anyone else.

Within hours, all of the spies had died from a plague – except for Joshua and Caleb.[2] Moses' urgent prayer to God had saved the rest of the nation from immediate and utter destruction,[3] but God had announced that none of those then over twenty would ever enter the Promised Land.[4] Instead, their children would enter the land,[5] there to be shown how easy it is to overcome giants when God is on your side.

As a result, the entire nation had been forced to turn back and wander the inhospitable wilderness for another 38 hopeless years.[6] After 15 of these years, Zelophehad had married Mother,[7] and the next year, their first daughter Noah had been born, followed by her sisters Mahlah, Hoglah, Milcah and Tirzah, one every two years, like clockwork.[8]

Soon after the birth of the youngest girl, Tirzah, Zelophehad's wife died. It was tragic, really, but she was

---

[2] Numbers 14:36-38

[3] Numbers 14:11-23

[4] Numbers 14:28-30

[5] Numbers 14:31

[6] Numbers 14:28-35. The forty years appears to have included the two years already spent in the wilderness since leaving Egypt (see Deuteronomy 2:14).

[7] We do not know the name of Zelophehad's wife.

[8] We do not know the order of birth or the age of any of the girls. Their names are listed four times in the Bible and each time Mahlah occurs first. Three times, Noah is second and Tirzah last, while on the other occasion, Tirzah is second and Noah last.

merely one of thousands of people dying at an early age throughout the nation, their bodies being hastily buried in scattered graves – graves that would never be revisited by grieving relatives once the nation had moved on to another campsite. Families were experiencing first-hand the cost of rejecting God's love and disobeying his commands.

Noah was almost nine years old when Mother died, and it was she who took over as the mother of the family, determined to give each of her sisters a family life they could be proud of. She took to mothering as a lamb takes to eating grass – with enthusiasm and long-term devotion.

When Noah was nineteen years old, her father Zelophehad also died, and then she became a fill-in father as well. Once again, she took on the job with whole-hearted devotion, the thought of marrying never entering her head. Her sisters still needed her: how else could they be cared for and prepared for marriage themselves?

It was as the 38 extra years of wandering in the wilderness were drawing to an end that Mahlah made the observation with which we started this story.

"I was just thinking," she said, and her sisters looked at each other.

"Oh, no!" they all answered.

As usual, Mahlah ignored this discouraging response and said, "We are all descendants of Jacob: a man. Our family is from the tribe of Manasseh: a man. Our father was from the Hepherites, and Hepher was the son of Gilead, the son of Machir, the son of Manasseh. All of the people in the list are men. The inheritance goes through sons; men. But Father had no sons. Does that mean his name will just drop out of the family? Disappear completely?"

The sisters looked at each other again, this time thoughtfully. Why hadn't that question occurred to anyone else? None of them wanted their father's name to disappear from the genealogical records. Father had not been perfect – and would have been horrified if anyone had suggested that he was – but he had been a pretty good Dad, and had never made them feel unimportant or unwanted because they were only girls and could not continue his name in the family.

Noah felt a little shocked. She had known their father better than any of the younger girls and knew that he had never complained about his "gaggle of girls", as he called them. Yet she also knew that family inheritance and lineage were important to him. He was proud to be a descendant of Joseph, the most famous of Jacob's sons. It had never occurred to Noah that he might be disappointed with their gender or with the plethora of girls God had given him. In thinking back over the days near the end of his life, though, she began to wonder if Mahlah's insight might explain some of the comments he had made. He had been accepting of what life had given him, but had still seemed a little disappointed in ways that Noah had not understood at the time.

Mahlah's thoughts came at a time when the people of Israel were beginning to look forward to finally being able to enter the Promised Land. Imagine it! Settling down to live in one place on land that would stay in the family for generations. Most of the nation had been born in the wilderness, born in tents, born to keep moving whenever and wherever the cloud of God led them. For this generation, that was life as normal – but it still inspired a longing to settle and build a family while living on the land.

But everyone knew that inheritance went through the men of the family. It was sad, but Zelophehad had missed out badly when he had all daughters and no sons.

At that moment, Noah and her sisters decided that they were not willing to allow that to happen without a fight. Father deserved that they at least make an effort to ensure that he didn't slip from the memory of the nation, the tribe or the clan.

They started the official wheels turning, and within days, the echoes of their question had reverberated even in the ears of Moses. A time was set for this extraordinary question to be considered by Moses, Eleazar the priest and the leaders of the congregation. It was to be an open hearing: anyone could be present to listen, and many took an interest in this strange situation.

The girls were called and given the opportunity to explain their problem, which they did simply and clearly.

Moses quickly understood the problem and could have given them the widely accepted answer: inheritance goes exclusively through sons, never through daughters. Yet he was uncomfortable with this because it condemned men like Zelophehad – blessed only with daughters – to exclusion from the tribal genealogies and inheritance. So he asked God for a judgement, and God's answer was clear and simple, although few expected it.

Once the nation was established in the land and the land was being assigned to individuals within their tribal areas, Noah and her sisters were to inherit the land their father would have received.

It was a fascinating conclusion, and those who liked to study God's character as it shone through his laws, happily added this extra fact to their understanding of Yahweh. Extra judgements were also provided for the case where men died, not only without sons, but without any children at all. Simplified, it all meant that the land must stay within a tribe, to be inherited by the closest available male relative.

The question had been answered and the tricky situation nicely straightened out. Zelophehad's daughters were known throughout the nation. Through their efforts, he was famous.

But more was yet to come.

Some time later, the girls were sitting and chatting together, Hoglah a little distractedly because her thoughts were occupied by a young man from the camp of Ephraim who had been paying her particular attentions recently.

"I was just thinking," began Mahlah, and this time the other girls contented themselves with looking at each other. Since the episode of the inheritance, the others had treated Mahlah's thoughts with a little more respect. After all, each of them was an heiress now, largely because of Mahlah's unusual thoughts.

"Since the judgement about our inheritance, we've all been a little more popular with the men than we were before. And Hoglah's latest conquest got me thinking, because he is not from the same tribe as we are. He is from Ephraim, not Manasseh. Now it seems to me that if Hoglah were to marry this young man, our father's place in Manasseh would be lost again, and the land she is to inherit would become a little island of Ephraim inside Manasseh. Now I have nothing against the tribe of Ephraim – as descendants of Joseph, they are our closest relatives, I suppose. But Manasseh's land should belong to his descendants."

There wasn't much need for discussion. Everyone agreed: Mahlah's thinking seemed to have uncovered a major problem.

Once again, it was Noah who pursued the matter, and within a short time, the leaders of their clan had taken up the question and arranged a hearing before Moses and the other leaders. This likewise was to be an open hearing, and many came to listen, intrigued by the story of these five girls.

The leaders of Manasseh explained the situation created by the special case of Zelophehad and his daughters. Everyone now knew that the girls were to inherit land when Canaan was conquered, but if they married men from other tribes, their land would be transferred to the other tribe and Manasseh would lose some of its inheritance.

Once more, these girls – and others like them in other tribes – would require special rules. Any girls who inherited land would, alone of all the girls in Israel, have to marry within their own tribe, so that the land they inherited would stay within their tribe.

The young man from Ephraim was disappointed, but, one by one, the girls found husbands among their cousins. One cousin was even courageous enough to marry Mahlah, braving her "I was just thinking" moments. Their first child was a daughter, which really got her thinking....

At last it was Noah's turn. The oldest, the one who had felt responsible for her sisters and had waited for all of them to be married, was finally free to be married herself.

Four

My son – given to God

For the true story, see 1 Samuel 1:1-2:21.

Now that Samuel is so famous as a prophet, people often ask me what he was like as a child and whether there really was anything special about his birth.

Of course, there *was* something special, but most of what was special was his mother – and her attitude.

The basic story that people tell about Samuel is all true, but there are a few details that generally get left out that I'd like to include as well.

When I was young, I met a wonderful girl: godly and altogether delightful. A while later, we married and were very happy together. After a few years of marriage, though, a cloud began to overshadow our happiness: we had no children.

Then my parents spoke to me and made a suggestion. I disregarded it at the time, but they worked on me over the next few months until finally I agreed to do what they suggested.

I wish that I hadn't.

Their suggestion was that I marry another woman in order to have a son to continue the family name.

Initially I felt that our having a child was something that was under God's control, and was nothing for *me* to worry about. Nevertheless, my parents pointed out that taking a second wife was not really so unusual, and I had to admit that they were right. They even had a woman in mind – the oldest daughter of a friend of the family. I wouldn't say that they had been having problems finding someone to marry her, but she certainly could be awkward at times.

My first wife, and the love of my life, was Hannah, and she was willing to go along with the plan if I thought it was best. I didn't, but continuing the family line *is* important and Hannah didn't seem to be able to have children.

So I married Peninnah, and from then on life was difficult. At first it wasn't too bad, although, as I said, Peninnah could be difficult at times. Then she had a child – which had, after all, been the point of the whole setup – and her behaviour towards Hannah became a source of real trouble in the family.

As she had more children over the years, her sneering at and teasing of Hannah became more and more pronounced. Peninnah also took every possible opportunity to try to turn me against Hannah. She constantly reminded me that *she* was the wife who had given me all my children. Not a week passed without her explicitly presenting her oldest son to me as my first and most important child. She criticised Hannah in so many different ways that I couldn't list them all if I tried. According to Peninnah, Hannah was not a real woman because she couldn't have children; she must be evil because God wouldn't give her children; and she had probably been unfaithful to me, which was why she couldn't have children. The attempts went on and on, and I didn't believe any of them. But, short of beating her into submission, I couldn't stop her saying them.

She even tried to convince me that Hannah was always rude and cruel to the children, but I knew Hannah too well to believe that either. I had watched Peninnah and Hannah carefully as the children grew, and there was no doubt that Hannah helped Peninnah and her children, while Peninnah constantly provoked and teased Hannah.

You may wonder why I kept Peninnah as a wife if she behaved like that, but she was my wife. I wasn't going to behave like the Gentiles and dispose of a wife just because she said things I didn't like. But how uncomfortable she made my life! Yet that was nothing compared to the cruelty with which she treated Hannah. My life was difficult, but Hannah's was far worse.

In those days I often found Hannah, the delight of my eyes, weeping because of Peninnah's actions or words.

All I could do was to wish that I had never married Peninnah. A happy marriage with no children would have been far better than having children and two wives who could never get along together.

I also need to point out that Hannah never, not even once, tried to turn me against Peninnah. Hannah knew that I loved her and could have used that love to make Peninnah suffer, but she didn't.

So when people ask me about the birth of Samuel, I always say that one of the special things about his birth was his mother and her attitude to God.

When we went to Shiloh each year for the feast, I always followed our normal custom and gave special presents to my wives and children, and every year the present I gave Hannah was twice as big as the present I gave Peninnah. It was meant to show that I loved her, but when I think back, I wonder whether it was a wise thing to do. It seemed only fair to give her something special when her rival always got presents both for herself and for her children – but maybe it was extra fuel on the fire of Peninnah's bullying nature.

The trouble was always worst at the feast, and each year it got worse, until Hannah would often weep and not eat. I couldn't jolly her out of it either.

One year everything came to a head. When I returned to our lodgings after making our offering to God, it was obvious that Hannah had been crying. Peninnah was looking pleased with herself, which left me in no doubt as to what had been happening.

I took Hannah into another room privately and spoke to her, but she was inconsolable. What is a man to do when his responsibilities cause such conflict? I felt so sorry for Hannah, but Peninnah was also my wife, for good or ill. How strongly I felt at that moment that my decision to take a second wife had been foolish, and that the woman I had chosen was a very bad choice indeed.

It was time for a meal and Hannah prepared it for us, but she herself was too upset to eat.

"Poor Hannah," said Peninnah in a sickly-sweet voice. "She's not feeling well – and no child to give her a cuddle."

"Stop it," I snapped, and I'm afraid my voice showed my anger. Peninnah said no more, merely smiling in a self-satisfied way and putting her arm around our oldest son.

Once the meal was finished, Hannah went by herself to the tabernacle, and what happened there is now deservedly famous.

When she returned, I was pleased to see that she was much happier. She immediately told me what had happened: that she had asked God for a son and that Eli had blessed her request. But she had also promised that, if God gave her the son she was asking for, she would give him to God for the rest of his life, and that concerned me for a number of reasons, which I'll try to explain. You see, I love and worship Yahweh our God, and have great respect for Eli too, but his sons are terrible men.

If God gave us a son and we dedicated him to God by giving him to the priests, what would happen to him? Eli was already old – if he died, what would happen to a young boy left to the tender care of his evil sons? And even at the best of times, would the priests want a young boy under their feet anyway? Dedicating a son to God sounded very nice, but I felt that sometimes we need to be practical. How wrong I was! God is much more practical than we are, and when he wants something, he makes it work – very practically.

However, this uncertainty that I felt left me with a difficult decision. Under Moses' law, if a wife makes a vow, her husband can annul it if he chooses to, but only if he does so on the day on which he hears about it.[9] I could tell that Hannah had made this commitment out of desperation and her love of God, and that she was deeply committed to fulfilling it – if God would give her a son. I could also tell

---

9 Numbers 30:6-15

that she was completely convinced that this was exactly what God would do.

This was no careless, unthinking vow, I knew that – but at the same time, I felt that it wasn't very practical and might even be dangerous, because of Eli's sons.

What should I decide?

Hannah had prayed a lot about the subject that day, and I decided to do the same. I also weighed up the pros and cons and tried to think through where each option might lead. All the while, I could see in my mind's eye the happy smile that had brightened Hannah's face when she returned from the tabernacle.

I'm quite certain *now* that my final decision was the right one, but it wasn't so simple at the time. I decided to support Hannah in her vow. After all, if we had a son, wasn't that proof that God was answering Hannah's prayer? God would choose whether or not he wanted a child given to him.

I also decided to make my own commitment – a vow to match Hannah's – so the next morning, I went to worship and made a vow of my own, a promise that I would fulfil if God gave us a son. Then we went home.

Not long afterwards, Hannah became pregnant, and you can imagine how excited we were by God's answer to prayer. Peninnah was disappointed, but we didn't let her attitude affect our joy. She suggested derisively that the child might be a girl, but of course it wasn't.

Hannah and I were both completely convinced that our son, Samuel, was given by God. For some reason, God wanted Samuel dedicated to him in a special way.

Soon after his birth, it was time to go to Shiloh again, and my practical soul was questioning again: would Eli want a 3-week old baby delivered to him to look after?

This time, Hannah had the most sensible suggestion: she was still feeding Samuel, and while that was the case he would need to stay with her. After that, he would go to Shiloh and be dedicated to God. I was satisfied with the idea as long as Hannah didn't get too attached to Samuel and end up unable to give him up.

That year, I went to Shiloh with only Peninnah and her children. She was much quieter and less aggressive than she had been the previous year. No longer being the only mother in the family seemed to improve her behaviour. In fact, Samuel's birth was the beginning of much greater harmony in our family, and of a permanent improvement in Peninnah's character.

I paid my vow to God, then reminded Eli of the woman he had seen praying the previous year and told him all about the wonderful gift Yahweh had given us. I thought it would be best to warn him about what was coming so that he wouldn't get a shock when we turned up at the feast with Samuel, expecting to dedicate him to God and leave him at the temple. I got the feeling that Eli was quite happy with the idea of having another chance to bring up children. By then his own sons were so evil that he had given up on them. I'm not completely surprised, but it would have been better if he had still tried to bring them under control.

Anyway, he had some ideas of different ways to bring up Samuel and teach him about God. I had heard lots of people reflecting on how Eli and his wife had brought up their children, and nobody had a single good word to say about either the methods or the results. The ideas he mentioned to me sounded much more sensible, which eased my worries a little.

After Hannah weaned Samuel, we took him with us to Shiloh, made sacrifices and presented Samuel to Eli. Such a delightful little toddler he was, quite tall for his age and with a smile just like his mother's. He has always looked at one with a straight, steady gaze, and that characteristic was already obvious when he was introduced to Eli. We had explained to him what was happening, and I felt that he was looking forward to seeing the tabernacle and Eli. Hannah had done her best to make the changes that were coming in his life as attractive as possible, and she succeeded. Oh, but it was hard saying goodbye to him when we left to return home to Ramah. He waved to us, and we waved to him, and then Hannah and I walked away. His absence left a big hole in our life which nothing could ever fill, but God showed his appreciation for our sacrifice by giving us three more sons and two daughters.

Peninnah died some years ago, and Hannah and I were both sorry. We have missed her company, something that would have been inconceivable before Samuel was born!

Hannah and I are now contentedly growing old together. Our sons and daughters are grown and most have children of their own, blessing us with grandchildren and happiness. Our most famous son is Samuel, but we believe that we would never have had any children if Hannah had not been willing to give him up.

Five

Obed-edom

For the true story, see 2 Samuel 6:1-15; 1 Chronicles 13:9-14; 15:1-16:3. For the background of how the ark was captured and taken to the land of the Philistines, was subsequently returned and stored in the house of Abinadab, see 1 Samuel 4:1-7:2.

I was there when Uzzah died. A tragic accident, and something that should never have happened.

King David is a wonderful king over Judah and Israel, and he was a magnificent leader even before that, but in this case, he was probably the one who made the mistake.

What a responsibility to bear! A king has so many people depending on him, and any mistake he makes can cost individuals so much.

Don't take this to be a criticism of David. He is very much a man after God's own heart, and I owe him everything good that I have in life.

I couldn't have done any better myself, because at the time I knew no more than anyone else about how Yahweh's ark should be treated. Now, though, I think that I know everything God has ever told his people about what they should do for his ark. In fact, I might know more than any natural-born Israelite. You see, I didn't want to die like Uzzah, or the men of Beth-shemesh, or my countrymen before them.

Yes, many people have died over the years because they have been careless with Yahweh's ark. But as far as I can tell, no-one has ever been hurt if they have been careful to obey the instructions that God has given about it. I am not an Israelite, but I have done my best to obey his rules in life – and particularly in regard to the ark of his covenant with Israel.

I first met David in my hometown, Gath. Saul, the king of Israel, was persecuting David in a way that just didn't make sense. In fact, it made so little sense that we in Gath used to call him "Crazy Saul" because of the way he behaved. One of the things that impressed me about David when I first got to know him was that he wouldn't ever use that name, or let us use it either. Imagine that, a foreign visitor who insisted that his hosts treat their enemy – and his – with respect! Yet David didn't seem to be worried that we might be suspicious of his motives or think that he was really on Saul's side. He had his standards and he didn't care who knew what they were.

Later I found that he was not quite as straightforward a character as I had thought, but he always had moral reasons for what he did. He didn't do things just for convenience or self-aggrandisement.

When David came to Achish at Gath, I was in Achish's army, and very suspicious of this wonder-boy from Israel. It seemed to me that he was probably a spy, sent to find out information about our army. But even if he wasn't a spy, he was still a real threat to those of us who were fighting for Achish. He was already famous for his bravery and remarkable leadership, so what would happen when he and his men joined our army? I wasn't the only one who was worried that he and his men would take all of the best jobs in Achish's army.

We tried to resist his influence, chip away at his credibility, question his behaviour, do anything that we could to slow him down and, if possible, get rid of him.

But as I got to know him, I liked what I saw. He turned out to be more religious than any other man I know, but he was religious in a practical sense. He didn't spend all of his time in temples worshipping; instead, he lived what he believed.

He was a virtuoso on any instrument he picked up: music just oozed out of him, and he could make a lyre sound as if it had suddenly realised what music was all about. There didn't seem to be any style of music that he couldn't make irresistible. Watching him play was a joy in itself, and hearing him sing his amazing poetry was beyond description.

Some soldiers do have skill with music, but on the whole, our words and music tend to be crude and clumsy – the sort of thing you might expect from people who are normally under the influence of wine when they make music!

David used music as a tool of exquisite sensitivity, and his tunes made even the best work of our Philistine composers seem heavy and ungainly. On an instrument, his hands moved with a gentleness, an airy caress that seemed completely at variance with the picture of a strapping war hero who had violently planted a rock between the eyes of

Goliath, our greatest champion, and then hacked off the man's head with his own colossal sword.

Yet it was neither the tunes nor the rhythms that made David's music so beautiful – it was the words he matched with them, and the perfect balance he achieved between joy and melancholy, praise and hope.

Even the most beautiful scene you have ever marvelled at is cold and empty without the haunting delight of David's exquisite melodies as he alone can coax them from a harp. Yet even with such ethereal music filling your heart with wonder, it is only with the addition of his poetry, sung in a throat-catchingly beautiful tenor, that you really begin to understand what is missing in life. David alone is able to show us how great a yearning man can have for fellowship with the eternal God of creation.

All of this, David could do, and I was blessed to meet him and learn from him about Yahweh, the God of Israel.

Of course, I wasn't the only one. David has convinced Hittites, Cushites, Ammonites, Jebusites and many others to believe in the one true God. It's just part of him, and he has never told us that we're not good enough to worship God. Some of his countrymen think that they are so special because God chose Israel, but David isn't like that at all. He talks of the promise God made to Abraham that God's people would be a blessing to all nations, and he really believes it. He wants us all to believe in Yahweh and love his laws.

While David was still living with Achish in Gath, I managed to wangle a position on his staff. By that time, I was convinced that Dagon and our other gods were nothing compared with Yahweh, and being in David's camp made it easier to avoid the religious festivals that I no longer felt comfortable with. It made things easier with my family too, because they wouldn't accept that I thought of Dagon as nothing but a lifeless idol.

When David moved to Ziklag, I went with him and was glad to cut off my connections with Philistia. I was sad to leave my family behind completely, but they hadn't given me any choice.

But I'd better skip over the years we spent in Ziklag and Hebron, and David's conquest of Jebus, or I'll never get to the part that really matters – and why it matters.

I stayed with David through all of that time, but I was really getting a bit old for fighting in the army, so when he moved to Jebus (and called it Jerusalem again), I took the opportunity to settle down. Since I knew from David that Jerusalem is special to God, it seemed the best place to live, and just living in the same city as David is encouraging anyway.

Then David came up with this plan of bringing the ark of the covenant to Jerusalem and putting it in a tent near his palace. It seemed a beautiful plan to me. As a Philistine – even before I got to know David – I had a great respect for the ark, since my people had tried to take it away from Israel as a trophy and thousands had lost their lives as a result.

I didn't know it then, but when God told Moses to build the ark, it wasn't just an ark that he was to build. He was also to build a tent for the ark to live in. The ark was to be the centrepiece of the whole tabernacle, which was really a portable temple for the Israelites to use in the wilderness while they were travelling to the promised land of Israel. The tent was to stand inside a curtain-walled courtyard, while the ark would stay inside an inner room of the tent. Only one man – the High Priest – was ever allowed to go into that inner room. That information alone should have shown everyone that they had to be very careful with the ark – it wasn't just a gold-plated box with some poles attached!

But the people of Israel had not looked after the ark properly at all – I know that now. They had used it more as a good-luck charm or a talisman, in the hope that it would win them battles. They had removed the ark from the tent and taken it to a battlefield, but, far from giving them good luck, Israel had lost the battle so badly that my people, the Philistines, got their hands on the holy ark.

It wasn't long before they wished they hadn't!

At that time my father was just a few years old and my grandfather was fighting in the army of the king of Gath. Over the next seven months, Yahweh attacked Dagon our god and brought such terrible plagues on my people that finally everyone was almost certain that the plagues couldn't be happening just by chance.

However, we all know that unusual things can still happen by chance, so somebody had the bright idea of putting the ark on a cart as a test. The clever bit was to yoke to the cart two cows that had never worn a yoke before, and were also still feeding their calves, which were locked up back in their stalls.

Ordinarily, utter confusion would result, as the two cows would have no idea how to pull together in a yoke, and anyway, they would both be fighting to get back to their calves!

It was a brilliant idea and a perfect test. If Yahweh was really controlling the plagues, then he should be able to control two upset cows – and that's exactly what he did.

My grandfather told me that when they let the cows go they immediately started walking together towards Beth-shemesh. Complete coordination and cooperation. But they didn't seem happy with it – they mooed and mooed as they walked, and wagged their heads backwards and forwards. Grandfather said that it was clear they wanted to be back with their calves, but an unseen hand was leading them along the road. Those are the very words he used: "an unseen hand". Yahweh was always treated with respect in my house when I was growing up. In fact, from the stories I've heard, it seems that many of us Philistines showed more respect for Yahweh than the people of Israel did at times!

Those cows just kept plodding all the way to Beth-shemesh, not turning to left or right, until they stopped near a huge stone where the Israelites of the town were harvesting their wheat. The harvesters were thrilled to see the ark, so they took it down from the cart, chopped up the cart and offered the two cows as burnt offerings.

At that stage, the lords of the Philistines gave up and went back home. They were all completely convinced that Yahweh *was* in control and that the plagues in our land had truly been his work. It helped to significantly reduce the tensions between the two nations for many years.

However, because they left then, they didn't see that God killed some of the men of Beth-shemesh because they looked into the ark. Once again, I don't want to be critical, but God had warned the Israelites not to do so hundreds of years before! Besides, Beth-shemesh is one of the towns that

Israel's priests were given to live in, so they of all people should have known how to treat the ark! But either they didn't know, or they chose not to obey – and more people died.

Some of Yahweh's commands are hard to keep – like the command to love one's neighbour as oneself, which is very hard with some neighbours! – but a simple collection of rules about how to treat a gold-plated wooden box shouldn't be that hard to obey. But you can only obey a command that you know about, and that is what the priests are meant to ensure. Yahweh's priests are meant to teach his nation the laws he has given. But over time, that knowledge has been forgotten because nobody seems to feel it is their personal duty to know. So, over the generations, more people keep dying because they choose ignorance over obedience.

After the people died in Beth-shemesh, they sent the ark to Kiriath-jearim, and it stayed in the house of a man named Abinadab for a long, long time – about twenty years before Saul became king, another forty years during his reign and then about eight years of David's reign before he decided to bring the ark into the City of David.

During all of that time – almost seventy years – I don't believe that anybody died because of the ark. Instead, Abinadab and his sons were careful to treat God and his ark with the proper care and respect.

David made plans for bringing the ark into Jerusalem with great celebration, but he made the mistake of following the ideas of the Philistines instead of the commands of God. I suppose that God accepted what we Philistines had done because we couldn't have known any better – but God's people had been told what to do and *should* have known and obeyed.

David provided a new cart that was pulled by oxen, and Uzzah died because he touched the ark when the oxen stumbled.

Yet God had specifically designed the ark with poles for *carrying* and had said that the ark was to be carried by men – priests – on their shoulders. Once you know what's right it's all so obvious, isn't it? After all, why else would the ark have poles?

God had said: "they must not touch the holy things, lest they die."[10] When I read those words from the books of the law, they struck me like a dagger-thrust. But that wasn't all – when carts were being allocated for carrying the parts of the tabernacle in the wilderness, none were given to the sons of Kohath because "they were charged with the service of the holy things that had to be *carried on the shoulder*."[11]

It was all there, including examples of the priests carrying the ark.[12] This was the vital information that would have saved Uzzah's life – all there for people to read, but no-one had bothered to do so.

You may wonder why an old soldier like me would start reading religious scrolls, and ones in Hebrew at that! When I was young, I was always more interested in physical action – often violent action – than reading. The truth is, it was fear that started me reading. I didn't want to die like Uzzah, or

---

[10] Numbers 4:15
[11] Numbers 7:9
[12] Deuteronomy 31:9; Joshua 3:3

the men of Beth-shemesh, or even my own countrymen so many years before.

And the fear came because, when Uzzah died, King David decided that my house was the best place to put the ark.

My house!

I think you can imagine the scene without me needing to describe it: the unexpected stopping of the cart; the sudden silence that descended on the crowd like a blanket, hard on the heels of the whispered explanations of what had happened; the terrified looks; the gasps of shock; the backward steps.

However, I was too close to see most of this. I had been standing at the door of my house and the cart had stopped right in front of me. Uzzah had been so full of life and happiness, taking such care that nothing could possibly happen to the precious cargo he was superintending. Then the oxen stumbled, he reached out a swift steadying hand, and suddenly he collapsed.

Not many people had seen what had happened, because most were watching their king dancing in joyous celebration – David himself took a while to realise that something was terribly wrong – but I had seen every step of the action from the moment the oxen stumbled. I was glad that I had – it meant that I could rule out the obvious suggestions and report that Uzzah's collapse had happened at the very instant that he had touched the ark. He had not been either run over or knocked down; no, this was the hand of God.

What tragic accidents come through ignorance.

For several moments, nobody went to Uzzah. The few who had seen what had happened felt the terror inspired by the destroying hand of God. But I was a soldier, and soldiers are used to helping their fellows whatever the danger, so I was the first to reach his side and roll him onto his back, trying to see how he was. I didn't feel that I was in any great danger, although I'd heard all the stories about the ark and its fatal power. Anyway, I couldn't just leave him lying on the road when he might need help. Ahio, his brother, arrived next and we examined Uzzah together.

It took only a few moments to find out that we couldn't do anything to help Uzzah, and by that time, the procession had stopped and David was running back towards us.

"What happened, Obed-edom?" he asked, breathlessly.

"Uzzah touched the ark. He's dead."

"Why?"

"The oxen stumbled and he tried to steady the ark."

"Has he ever collapsed before, Ahio?"

"No," said Ahio, "but this was no normal fainting or anything like that."

"But God wouldn't kill anyone like this. We were honouring him. Honouring his ark. Praising him."

Nobody answered. The facts spoke for themselves – Uzzah was dead.

"We had all the plans made," David continued, and it was easy to hear the anger growing in his voice. "Thousands of people have gathered today to celebrate bringing God's ark into Jerusalem. Why did Uzzah touch the ark? He has caused so much trouble and ruined all of our plans."

David continued to express his anger, and most of it was aimed at Uzzah, but in that mood, some of it was also directed at God. I've never been one to argue with David because he has so much more wisdom and intelligence than I have, but this time I spoke up: "You would have done the same, sir."

"What do you mean?"

"He saw the ark rocking and thought he needed to steady it. I would have done the same – and so would you, sir."

"And now he's dead."

"Yes, sir."

"Well, I suppose you're right – if I had been there I would have done just what he did. And I would have been dead."

"Yes, sir, I think so."

"How can the ark of God come to me if anyone who is near it can be struck dead at any time?"

"But haven't Uzzah's family had the ark in their house for many years? Has anyone died during that time?"

"No."

"Then it must be something that we did differently today."

"Well, whatever it was, we can't move the ark any further now, and that's flat." I had seen David in many battles and was familiar with his indomitable courage, but now the fear in his voice was palpable. "Is this your house, Obed-edom?"

"Yes, sir," I said slowly.

"We can't leave the ark here on the road, so we'll need to put it on your property for a while until we work out what to do. Be careful, Obed-edom."

So that was how the ark and its cart ended up being driven onto my land, just as they carried away the body of poor Uzzah.

David called the priests and they covered the ark. Everybody was far too afraid to touch it, so some material was draped over it without anyone getting very near it. Even so, everyone was very glad once the operation was over and the ark was sitting right next to my house.

Everyone except me.

I felt a strange mix of terror and elation.

Before the end of the day, I made sure that the cart and the ark were covered with a roof. I couldn't leave the ark of God out in the weather – it didn't seem right – but I was very, very careful not to touch the ark as I rigged up that roof.

King David arranged for several priests to guard the ark to keep it safe, and that got me thinking. It was fine to "be careful" with the ark, but did anyone actually *know* what was right and what was wrong in dealing with the ark? I spoke to the priests who were on guard, and they gave me the hint I needed by saying that instructions had been given, but that nobody knew them anymore – it had been unnecessary because the ark hadn't been moved for so long.

The next day, the priests arranged for me to read the scriptures. Not only were they surprised that I would *want* to read them, they also weren't sure that foreigners should be *allowed* to read them. If David hadn't been king, I doubt that I would have been given permission, but he has always insisted that Yahweh welcomes people of any nation who are determined to worship him. Of course, there are still limitations on how foreigners can worship depending on which nation we come from. In this case, though, the priests agreed that I could read Moses' writings of the law of God. I read through them all diligently, and whenever I came across any instructions about the ark, I copied them down on a scroll of my own so that I would know exactly what was and what was not allowed. Shortly afterward, I felt confident that I knew what had gone wrong for Uzzah, and was careful to follow the instructions myself by not looking into or touching the ark. It was just that simple! Uzzah's life would have been saved if only he had known God's commands and obeyed them.

Since then, the ark has stayed safely at my house, covered and kept dry. No-one has touched it. No-one has died. On the contrary, God has blessed me and my household. It's amazing: everything we do is successful and every decision we make is right.

ℝ

After three months it has become obvious to everyone that God has been blessing me and my household. So now the priests have also been studying the law to find out what is required to move the ark to where King David wants it.

I've learned – and I hope that Israel as a nation has also learned – two very simple lessons from that tragic day:

1. if we don't know God's commands, we can easily disobey them without knowing it, and

2. if we disobey God, we are in great danger!

Ignorance of God's commands cost Uzzah his life, and it could easily have been anyone else who died instead – even King David.

Yet it really didn't take much for me to learn what God required, and obeying his commands hasn't been hard either. And with that obedience has come the blessings of the loving God of Israel about whom David has taught me so much.

Six

The God of Big Things

by Cathy Morgan

For the true story, see 1 Kings 17-19.

I always thought of God as the God of big things: nations and armies; earthquakes, floods and other disasters. After all, he is infinite and all-powerful! I've only gradually come to realise that he is a God of small things too.

Of course, it should have been obvious: a quick look at a flower or an insect shows such amazing design and complexity that it is obvious that the creator took pains with even the smallest of details in his work.

But I have always seen his hand in the big things. Looking back through history, the things he has done for us as his nation have always been big things: the plagues in Egypt, dividing the Red Sea and the Jordan, everything that happened at Mount Sinai, conquering the nations of Canaan – the list never ends. And that's not counting all that he has done to try to keep the nation on track, worshipping him and him only!

To this day, I'm not sure whether the plan was my own idea or given by God. From the fact that it failed, I have often concluded that I must have been mistaken in thinking God put the idea into my head, but when I think back on all the encouragement God has given his people in the past to make the same choice, only to have them turn away so often, I just don't know. But I'm getting ahead of myself.

Wherever the idea originated, I began praying for a drought, to get the people's attention so that they would turn back to God, convinced of his power shown by first stopping the rain and then sending it again. Then one day, God told me to go to King Ahab and warn him that there would be no dew or rain for some unstated number of years – in fact, until *I* said so.

Not a popular message, as you can imagine!

That was the first occasion on which I had to run for my life, and God directed me to a brook and made sure I was fed (in an obviously miraculous way[13]) until it dried up. A sign that he cared? I should have taken it that way, but I considered that it was just God protecting his prophet so that I could do the job he had for me, rather than thinking that he was taking care of me as a person. Even when he sent me to the widow, looked after our food supply and raised her son

---

[13] Well, have you ever had a large bird land right in front of you and stalk right up to you, doing its best to give you a small loaf of bread it's been carrying in its beak? My eyes nearly popped out of my head the first time it happened, even though God had warned me that he had told the ravens to feed me. I don't know where they got the food since they couldn't tell me! – but although I found it off-putting at first, eating something that had been in a bird's beak, we grew quite friendly over time. Soon, they would land on my hand and then hop to my knee, where they sat and let me pat them while I ate the bread and meat they brought – feeding them bits as I went, as payment. I was actually sorry to leave them when God sent me to Zarephath.

to life again, I still didn't see God's loving care in our individual lives. A lifelong mindset is hard to change.

The famine made things hard for everyone, even those being specifically cared for by God, like I and my adopted family were. Soon, food was running short for both people and livestock, and so was water in many places. It was a relief when God finally spoke to me again and told me to go to Ahab because rain was coming. But even through the worst of the famine, I clung to the hope that this proof of God's control over the weather, and the further signs he would be showing before sending rain, would be enough to bring the people back to him. So, it was with a heart full of hope that I returned to Israel.

I found Ahab out in the countryside – safely away from Queen Jezebel – and told him to arrange for all the people to gather on Mount Carmel on a given day, with the prophets of Baal and Asherah there as well. It was time for a showdown.

There was plenty of time for thought and prayer in those days of waiting as the messengers went all over the land to call the people to Mount Carmel, but I never really thought that the people *could* turn away from God once the difference between the true God and the Baals had been shown as plainly as I knew it would be.

At last the day came. A huge crowd met on Mount Carmel, forming a big circle in a bit of a natural amphitheatre, with the prophets in the middle. All of the prophets: eight hundred and fifty prophets of false gods, and one prophet of the true God. It was a lonely position to be in, but knowing that an all-powerful God was at my side was comforting. Although it was only me against 850 others, I was the one who made the rules for the contest and nobody argued. (Incidentally, King Ahab's attitude toward prophets of God has always puzzled me. The woman he married kills them whenever she gets the chance, but he himself seems happy to listen and even respond when given a message from Yahweh – at least until Jezebel steps in. A weak man, probably, with some respect for God, but more for his wife.) Regardless, in this case, what I said went. Two bulls were to be brought, one for them and one for me. Each side would build an altar, and whichever god sent fire from heaven to burn up the sacrifice would be acknowledged as the true God. I emphasised that the Israelites needed to make a decision which god to follow, and stick to it.

As there were so many more of them, I directed them to go first. They slaughtered their bull and placed it with some wood on the altar they had built, and then they started calling on Baal. They continued to call on him for hours, dancing around his altar. We had started early in the morning, but by noon they had still had no response. No surprise, of course. In fact, the whole thing struck me as rather funny, so I started teasing them: "Maybe he can't hear you because he's asleep! Or maybe he's going to the toilet..." Then they got more desperate, and the blood flowed from the cuts they made in their bodies in a frantic attempt to get their god's attention.

They kept limping around the altar, raving to their god, until the time of the evening sacrifice. Then I called an end to it. It was time to show the power of a real God. Turning away from the sorry-looking false prophets, I called the people to me and gathered twelve stones to repair God's altar. As they watched, I dug a trench around the base of the altar, then placed the wood on the altar and the bull on top. I wanted to show that nothing could stop God's work, so I got four men to fill four jars with water, and empty them over the altar; once, twice, three times, until the wood was soaked and the trench full. Although I had announced that God would be sending rain, water would remain a precious commodity until he had done so, so I don't know what the people thought about this 'wasting' of water. But it made my point: it had to be obvious to everyone that there was *no way* that anything on that altar could catch fire!

Once that was done, I blocked out the crowds that surrounded me and focussed only on God as I prayed aloud, "O Lord, God of Abraham, Isaac, and Israel, let it be known this day that you are God in Israel, and that I am your servant, and that I have done all these things at your word. Answer me, O Lord, answer me, that this people may know that you, O Lord, are God, and that you have turned their hearts back."

Well, the next instant there was the most dramatic and sudden response that I've ever had to a prayer – and one that confirmed my impression of God as a God of big things. Fire fell from heaven and completely consumed the bull, but it didn't stop there. It also consumed the wood, the stones, all that water, and even the surrounding dust! There was no way that anyone could doubt God's power, or explain away the miracle. And they didn't try. Instead, they all cried, "The Lord, he is God; the Lord, he is God." It had worked! The people were finally acknowledging Yahweh our God as the one true God.

Striking while the iron was hot, I ordered that all of the prophets of Baal and Asherah should be taken down to the brook Kishon and executed. Everyone joined in enthusiastically, and I felt that everything was going as I had hoped. Now for the last phase, I thought. I advised Ahab to have his meal while he could, and then headed up to the very top of the mountain to pray for rain.

Kneeling on the summit, I begged God to send the rain for which the land had been thirsting for so long. Sending my servant to look out to sea and scan the horizon for clouds, I continued to pray. As he returned again and again without news, I prayed still more fervently, until finally, the seventh time, he reported a cloud on the horizon, only the size of a man's hand. Knowing that my prayer was answered, I sent him again to Ahab, this time to warn the king to leave the mountain before the rain stopped him. I myself stood and watched the sky rapidly grow black with clouds – a beautiful sight after so long without rain.

❦

I wasn't left to watch the clouds for long because God's hand came upon me and I ran to Jezreel, racing Ahab in his chariot through the growing darkness and arriving at the gates of the city just before him. The power of God is incredible when it empowers you like that! King Ahab entered the city, but I didn't – I knew Queen Jezebel was in there, and she is a terrifying and vicious woman. I hoped that the king would be able to convince her that Yahweh was the one true God, not the false gods she worshipped and had brought with her from Sidon into Israel when she married him. I tried to imagine how she would respond when Ahab told her about her 850 dead prophets, but my imagination wouldn't stretch that far.

The next morning I was full of excitement and optimism as I watched the life-giving rain continue to fall – rain that proved God's power over not just fire, but water as well.

Surely all the people *must* turn back to God now! The killing of the false prophets on the mountain had been only the beginning of the work that was needed to clear the land of the idols that littered it. The first and most important step would be the silencing or removal of Jezebel, the foreigner who had led her husband and the rest of the nation further into idolatry. Though I was aware that this might not be easy, I was still hopeful that, after all Ahab had seen, he would have started working on convincing her as soon as he had returned to the palace. I knew that the land would never turn from idols to the true God as long as Jezebel was allowed to keep running the kingdom the way she had been doing.

Then, as I was praying and meditating on this, a message was delivered that completely destroyed my hopes and changed the course of my life. The message was from Jezebel. As expected, she had been told by her husband about the previous day's events, but the outcome had not been at all what I had hoped for. I had known Ahab to be a weak man, but I had thought that he would have at least some authority over his wife, and that the previous day's events would have had a major impact on him. Sadly, Jezebel's message showed this to have been wishful thinking. It was short and to the point: "So may the gods do to me and more also, if I do not make your life as the life of one of them by this time tomorrow." Her favourite prophets were dead and she was vowing to revenge herself on me.

A failure. My plan was a failure. I was a failure. Even after all those years as God's prophet, I still hadn't managed to turn the people back to him. If an exhibition of God's power like that shown on Mount Carmel couldn't convince the king then nothing would – and without the king's support, nothing would change. Even worse – from the point of view of my survival – Jezebel was still in control, and was planning to kill me.

I ran.

I headed south, hurrying first to escape from the land of Israel, and then continuing south through Judah too. By then I felt safer, but still just as much of a failure. My prayer was for death. "It is enough; now, O Lord, take away my life, for I am no better than my fathers." I had completely given up.

Yet instead of killing me, God sent an angel to give me two special meals, and to tell me that I would need the strength for my journey. It was a long way – all the way to Mount Sinai, the place where my people had met with God so many years before. The journey gave me plenty of time to think about how badly I had failed.

When I arrived, I found a cave to stay in while I waited for God to speak to me. Somehow, I was sure that he would. And he did. "What are you doing here, Elijah?" he asked.

Glad for the chance to voice my complaint, I replied, "I have been very jealous for the Lord, the God of hosts. For the people of Israel have forsaken your covenant, thrown down your altars, and killed your prophets with the sword, and I, even I only, am left, and they seek my life, to take it away."

Have you ever noticed that complaints often seem petty when they are stated out loud – however strongly they may be felt? I wanted to explain how I really felt, the mission I had had and how much I felt like a failure, but it just wouldn't come out. What did come out provided no real explanation of my earlier request that God take away my life. But God made no direct response to my words anyway. Instead, he told me to come out of the cave onto the mountain and stand before him. A scary thought, but I obeyed.

Almost without warning, a strong wind struck the mountain – the sort of grand phenomenon I've always seen God's hand in. But this time I knew that God was not in the wind, although it was so strong that it split the rocks of the mountain near me.

A fierce earthquake followed, and again, I knew that God was not in the earthquake. Yet I knew that he was in control of it, which prevented me from sinking to the ground in utter terror.

Then a fire came. But God was not in that either. I had seen God's hand in the fire on Mount Carmel, but now God was not in the fire.

Finally, after all the big things God had showed me, came something that I almost missed – a still, small voice. But there was no doubt it was God's voice, however small. It asked, again, "What are you doing here, Elijah?"

Somewhat confused by these events that had turned my thinking on its head, I could only repeat my earlier response: "I have been very jealous for the Lord, the God of hosts. For the people of Israel have forsaken your covenant, thrown down your altars, and killed your prophets with the sword, and I, even I only, am left, and they seek my life, to take it away."

Probably because he knew that this was not really what I meant, God made no attempt to answer me. Instead, he gave me instructions that would free me from the job for which I now felt so wholly inadequate: "Go, return on your way to the wilderness of Damascus. And when you arrive, you shall anoint Hazael to be king over Syria. And Jehu the son of

Nimshi you shall anoint to be king over Israel, and Elisha the son of Shaphat of Abel-meholah you shall anoint to be prophet in your place. And the one who escapes from the sword of Hazael shall Jehu put to death, and the one who escapes from the sword of Jehu shall Elisha put to death. Yet I will leave seven thousand in Israel, all the knees that have not bowed to Baal, and every mouth that has not kissed him."

I say that he made no attempt to answer me, but his last words did at least comfort me with the knowledge that, although others had not stood up publicly for God in the contest on Mount Carmel, apparently they did worship him in private. But that was a piece of information to mull over later. At the time, I focussed on the relief of knowing that the intolerable load of responsibility that I felt as a prophet of God was to be taken away and placed on the shoulders of another who would be better able to carry it.

And that was the end of the brief interlude on Mount Sinai. I had to go back to Israel as a prophet, but only to prepare my replacement. I was given no promise of protection from Jezebel's fury, but it no longer mattered. God had put things in perspective for me. He had reminded me of his power over everything through his control of the wind, fire and earthquake. God has given us all free will, and the fact that most choose to disobey is neither his failure nor mine. But it was the still, small voice that epitomised his main message to me. God is in control of the big things, and he uses them to work his will, but it is in the small things, and the small people, that his most magnificent work occurs. I hadn't even known about those seven thousand faithful men – but God had. And though he has chosen a nation to be his servant and witness, he works daily with any individuals who will listen to him.

Somehow, the knowledge that God does work in the small things, and cares for individuals, has made all the difference to me. I had gone to Mount Sinai afraid, lost and on the point of giving up. But the realisation that God cared brought everything into perspective. I was ready once more to work for God in whatever way he might direct me. As the God of both big things and small things, he can see the big picture clearly, while working with the little people in gentle love.

Seven

What I have vowed, I will pay

by Cathy Morgan

For the true story, see the book of Jonah.

I was just walking away from the temple when suddenly my eyes nearly popped out of my head. There, walking toward me, was a man I had mourned as dead, and, what's worse, by my hand: Jonah!

You see, it was like this. We were just about to weigh anchor in Joppa on our last voyage to Tarshish when a man came running up and asked if he could go with us to Tarshish. Naturally, I was rather suspicious of his motives, given the hurry he seemed to be in – we're respectable sailors, and want no part in helping criminals escape the law. But he explained that he hadn't broken the law, he was merely running away from his god. Now maybe that should have been a bit of a red flag, but I grew up in a culture with lots and lots of gods, and frankly, none of them seemed much worth worrying about. Of course, one does hear some strange things at times about the god of Israel, but if he was only running away from his own god that seemed like his business, not ours.

Anyway, that seemed no reason to deny him a passage, so he came aboard and paid his fare – the money was welcome – then he went below to keep out of our way. (Incidentally, I wonder whether I should be refunding his money? He didn't really get the passage he paid for....) Being out of the way, we forgot about him as the weather suddenly turned nasty and soon we were hard put to it to stay afloat. It was so bad that we even started throwing our cargo overboard to lighten the ship!

It was while we were bringing up the cargo from the hold, though the wild gyrations of the boat made the job difficult, that we were reminded of Jonah again. We found him fast asleep in a corner of the hold. Asleep! In that storm! Well, we woke him and brought him up on deck to call on his god. We were already calling on ours, but more gods had to be better, right? But this time it didn't help. Instead, the storm just kept getting worse.

It got so bad that some of the men started saying that it was no ordinary storm, and must have been sent by the gods because of something one of us had done. I was rather sceptical, but finally agreed to cast lots to see whose fault it was. Bits of straw of all different lengths were lying around in my cabin, so we collected one for each of us and I held them as each man in turn picked one out of the bunch. And who do you think picked the shortest straw? Our passenger, Jonah!

The next question was, what had he done? Well, he was quite open about the storm being his fault – he said he was a Jew, and worshipped the God who had made the whole world, hence his power over the storm. He, Jonah, had chosen to disobey this God and try to run away, and this was his punishment. But his remedy was one that none of us could accept. Well, how would you feel about throwing a man overboard? If a man falls overboard accidentally, we go to great lengths to try to recover him – so how could we throw someone in deliberately? Instead, we tried everything we could think of, even trying to row back to shore, but the storm just kept getting worse. Finally, we had to acknowledge that Jonah's suggestion was our only possible hope: to delay any longer would kill all of us, and still not save him. So we prayed to Jonah's God, begging forgiveness for what we were about to do in taking Jonah's life, and then over the side he went.

We were given no time to reconsider – Jonah instantly vanished under the water, and at the same instant, the most amazing miracle happened: the storm vanished, the sun shone, and the sea was as smooth as a mirror! If that's not an answer to prayer, I don't know what is. Well, there was only one possible response to such a miracle: we offered a sacrifice to Jonah's God, and made vows.

Because we had thrown all of the cargo overboard, we had to put back into port and load up again, but there was no chance to fulfil our vows then. Instead, they had to wait until we returned – by which time I think most of the others had forgotten about the whole thing. But I kept my vows in mind throughout our voyage, and travelled to God's temple to pay them as soon as we landed back in Israel.

So here I am, in Jerusalem at last, after a voyage that was peaceful other than a niggling feeling of guilt over the memory of having sent someone to their death. Though the others might have forgotten their vows made in the aftermath of the storm, I had to come and worship the one God who had showed himself to be truly powerful.

And God has rewarded me by taking away my guilt about Jonah. When I first saw him I doubted my eyes for a moment, until he caught sight of me and stopped short, looking momentarily uncertain whether he should slink away and hide, pretend he hadn't seen me or maybe even run up and greet me. I guess it would be kind of embarrassing to meet someone whom you'd got in such trouble that they'd had to throw you overboard. Seeing that the recognition was mutual, I cried out, "Jonah! But – but I thought you were dead...?"

Still with that slight reluctance, he approached me and explained stiffly that he was going to the temple to pay a vow he had made after his own deliverance from death. Not wanting to let him get away that easily, I asked, "Well, can we meet somewhere afterwards? I'd love to hear what happened to you."

He finally agreed, and we set a time to meet back at the temple steps. In what follows, I'll report his story in my own words, to avoid the confusion that might result if I reported our conversation verbatim, consisting as it did of probing questions on my part and evasive answers on his. He seemed (understandably) rather ashamed of his behaviour in various parts of his narrative, though I dare say I would have done no better.

The reason why Jonah had been on our ship in the first place was that he had been told by God to go to Nineveh to warn them of impending destruction. Like all of the other nations everywhere, he hated and feared the cruel Assyrians, and, naturally, would have preferred their immediate, well-deserved destruction to the probable future destruction of Israel at their hands. Why – believing in God's power as he did – he ever thought he could just run away like that and get away with it, is something that he was quite unable to explain. Maybe he thought that the delay would use up the time of grace that God had allowed for Nineveh. Anyway, run away he did – but get away with it he didn't!

On board our ship, he had known that God must have sent the storm, and had been willing to sacrifice his life for ours, knowing that he was responsible. But God had had other plans. Deep, deep down into the water he had plunged, until suddenly he became aware of a huge dark shape making for him. With no way to escape, he was swallowed whole by the monster. I couldn't get any description of his time inside the fish, beyond the statement, "It was dark – pitch dark – and slimy. There seemed no hope, but I couldn't believe that God had done this for no reason. There was nothing else I could do, so I spent a lot of time praying – and then praying some more." With no way of measuring time, it was only later that he discovered that he had been in the fish for three whole days and nights.

His exit from the fish was another thing that he said he preferred to forget. The sudden bright sunlight had been quite painful after all that time in unbroken darkness, but the fresh air had been such a welcome relief that it thoroughly outweighed the discomfort. The vows that he had made while in the fish were about to send him to Jerusalem when God intervened: "Go to Nineveh and preach there the message that I tell you." There was no avoiding this task, any more than there had been any way of escape from the fish by his own power.

This time he knew that he had no choice but to go, so he went. "Yet forty days and Nineveh will be destroyed!" The message was preached all over the city, reluctantly but thoroughly. Unfortunately – as he viewed it – he had all the success in preaching that he had expected, and that any prophet might envy. He got the undivided attention of the whole city, from the king down. They all repented, fasted and put on sackcloth, and then God relented. Suddenly Jonah's message was no longer needed – and no longer even true!

Jonah was out of a job, and was forced to accept that he had saved Israel's enemies from destruction. He left the city and sat down outside to watch, in the hope that God would see something he didn't like and go back to his original plan of treating the Ninevites as they deserved. But God showed him, using a plant and a worm, that the people in the city were important to God, and should likewise be important to Jonah.

Jonah glossed over what he did after that, and I didn't press him, seeing that he obviously wasn't happy with the subject and feeling that I had the basic story anyway. Eventually, though, he ended up in Jerusalem, fulfilling the vows he had made in the fish – just in time to meet me as I came to pay my own vows, and to set my mind at rest at the same time.

Such an ending! Only an all-knowing, all-powerful God could have arranged such circumstances, for, in bringing me to a belief in God, Jonah's defiant flight had saved a man from death, after which his grudging obedience had saved a whole city.

Eight

The Prophetess and the Book

For the true story, see 2 Kings 22:8-23:3; 2 Chronicles 34:14-32.

"*...And as the Lord took delight in doing you good and multiplying you, so the Lord will take delight in bringing ruin upon you and destroying you. And you shall be plucked off the land that you are entering to take possession of it.*" Shaphan the Secretary paused in his reading and looked at the king. Josiah was sitting on the stairs of the royal dais on which his ornate throne stood. His knees were bent up in front of him and his arms wrapped around them. His forehead rested on his knees. The purple robe he wore was worthy of a king, but as silence fell, Josiah lifted his head and with both hands grasped the neckline of the robe. Tears rolled down his cheek as he tore the expensive robe down to his waist. He continued to sit dejectedly in front of his throne, shaking his head.

"This is disastrous," he said, still shaking his head. "Catastrophic. We have all disobeyed God, and these curses will be coming on us as a nation," he said and his tears showed genuine remorse.

"But, my lord, you have always tried to serve Yahweh our God. How can you say that you have sinned?"

"There have been many things that have pricked my conscience as you have read, Shaphan, but there was one above all others that everyone in the entire nation has failed with. You read that we must attend three feasts each year in Jerusalem. We have not done that. They are meant to be feasts for joyfully celebrating God's blessings, yet we have ignored them all. Three feasts each year and I have never attended even one! That is sin, and God says that anyone who does not attend those feasts should be cut off from the nation. I have failed and there is nothing that can fix my failure." The young king lowered his head once more, obviously very upset and deep in thought.

"Shall I stop reading, my lord?" asked Shaphan, sympathetically. "It doesn't seem to get any better."

The king looked up again. "Are we absolutely sure that this book is genuine?" he asked. "Is it really the Book of the Law of Yahweh?"

"It appears genuine, my lord. The lettering is consistently genuinely ancient, the ink is faded in a way that seems to match, and the leather feels old too. Every aspect of this scroll that I can think of that could confirm its veracity fits. As a scribe I have had experience with many ancient scrolls over the years. I am convinced that this scroll is ancient. Hilkiah the High Priest is also convinced that it is genuine."

"Then I must hear it all, however unpleasant its message is."

"Very well, sire." Shaphan held up the scroll again.

"How much is there still to read?" asked the king.

"About a sixth."

"Let's keep going then."

"And the Lord will scatter you among all peoples, from one end of the earth to the other, and there you shall serve other gods of wood and stone, which neither you nor your fathers have known. And among these nations you shall find no respite, and there shall be no resting place for the sole of your foot, but the Lord will give you there a trembling heart and failing eyes and a languishing soul. Your life shall hang in doubt before you. Night and day you shall be in dread and have no assurance of your life. In the morning you shall say, 'If only it were evening!' and at evening you shall say, 'If only it were morning!' because of the dread that your heart shall feel, and the sights that your eyes shall see."

Josiah lowered his eyes again, shaking his head once more. Many of the details in the book had challenged his ideas of what God wanted, but the list of curses Shaphan was now reading was heaping horror upon horror. It felt completely unreal. How could things ever be bad enough for God to do such things to the nation he had chosen?

He, Josiah, was king. No-one but himself could take responsibility for his nation or feel more heavily the burden of the nation's failures. Yet now was not the time to ponder the meaning of all he had heard. First he must hear the remainder of the book so that all of the information was available for review. He must concentrate.

Shaphan continued reading and the terrible list of curses finally concluded. Yet the litany of terror was not finished. Some time later, as the Secretary neared the end of the scroll, he paused for a moment and looked at his king in sympathy, then read: *"I call heaven and earth to witness against you today, that I have set before you life and death, blessing and curse. Therefore choose life, that you and your offspring may live, loving the Lord your God, obeying his voice and holding fast to him, for he is your life and length of days, that you may dwell in the land that the Lord swore to your fathers, to Abraham, to Isaac, and to Jacob, to give them."*

Shaphan lowered the scroll and rolled it up.

"That's it, my lord," he said. "There was certainly a sting in the tail there." He shook his greying head.

"How *can* we choose life?" asked Josiah. "Through our actions, we have already chosen death. What can we do now?"

"Sire, the kingdom has already lasted for many, many years. Why should anything change now? If God has not destroyed us before now, why should he do so now?"

"But the punishment threatened in this book matches the punishment that prophets like Jeremiah have been telling us is coming."

"Ah yes, Jeremiah. He is busy in some other country somewhere, isn't he?"

"Yes, I believe he is. After all, he is a prophet for other nations too, not just Judah. Now, both Hilkiah and you agree that this book is genuine. This book threatens the kingdom with destruction. Is there anything that we can do to avert God's anger?

"You would have to ask a prophet that, sire... or maybe a prophetess."

"Yes, you're right. Maybe a prophetess. I have confidence in Huldah. She is a genuine messenger of Yahweh, and she won't be afraid to tell me the truth. Call

Hilkiah, Achbor, Asaiah and your son Ahikam. I want to speak to you all."

"Yes, sire."

❧

It wasn't long before the men Josiah had named were standing before him in the throne room. Shaphan had already briefed them on the situation, and they had all noticed the king's torn robe and dishevelled appearance.

"I want you all to go to see Huldah, the prophetess," said Josiah.

"Will you be coming with us, sire?" asked Achbor.

"No. I am too ashamed to present myself before God's prophetess. I am king, and am therefore responsible for my kingdom, which has not followed God's laws. I want you all to go and ask her about the Book of the Law."

❧

Later that afternoon, the group went to see Huldah, the prophetess of Yahweh. Her husband was the keeper of Josiah's wardrobe and they lived in what was called the second quarter – a part of the city that lay to the west of the old city of David, enclosed by new walls that had been built by Hezekiah and strengthened by Manasseh his son.

As Shaphan and his fellows walked along the street, doors opened and the inhabitants watched with interest as the cream of the kingdom's leaders trooped past. By the time the lords stopped outside the door of Huldah's house, they had accumulated quite a following of small children who rarely saw such elegant clothing.

The house in front of which they stopped was not large, and a critical observer could have guessed that the money that must have been spent on the visitors' clothing could have bought a much larger dwelling in a much nicer part of town. The visitors looked uncomfortable, to say the least, but they were a determined group of men, and the king's commands must be obeyed.

The door opened, and a middle-aged woman looked at the assembled lords. She did not seem surprised to see them.

"Welcome," she said.

"Is this the house of Huldah the prophetess, the wife of Tikvah?" asked Hilkiah, formally, in a deep, pleasant voice. This was essentially a religious matter, so who else but the High Priest should take charge?

"Yes it is, and I am Huldah. Welcome to my home. King Josiah sent you with an important request."

Hilkiah looked surprised, and stumbled a little in his explanations. "Ah, yes. The king sent us to you. It is a great honour that he pays you. He believes that you are a prophetess who can give him answers from God."

"He sent you to ask about the words he has read in the Book of the Law." She turned to Shaphan. "You did well to read the book to the king, my lord. It was just the right thing to do."

"Once I had started, the king insisted that I keep reading, right to the very end," said Shaphan with a wry smile. "It was a long job... and it upset the king greatly."

"Which is why we have come," said Hilkiah, taking back the baton of conversation. "The king is concerned that Yahweh's anger is like a great fire against us because our fathers have not obeyed the words of the book." Hilkiah was reporting King Josiah's message accurately, but his delivery of the words suggested that he did not have the same strength of conviction as his king.

Huldah's eyes were the most striking part of her appearance. She looked back at Hilkiah, and her eyes showed none of the servility that one might have expected from the wife of a fairly minor servant of the king when speaking to five of the most important men in the kingdom.

"Thus says the Lord, the God of Israel," she began. " 'Tell the man who sent you to me, Thus says the Lord, behold, I will bring disaster upon this place and upon its inhabitants, all the words of the book that the king of Judah has read. Because they have forsaken me and have made offerings to other gods, that they might provoke me to anger with all the work of their hands, therefore my wrath will be kindled against this place, and it will not be quenched.' "

Huldah paused and looked around at her audience. Her expression was firm and, like her words, brooked no argument. What the five lords thought in detail we cannot say, but the High Priest, Hilkiah, looked shocked. A look of anger filled Asaiah's face, while Shaphan seemed unsurprised, but not necessarily worried. Possibly he was not convinced.

After a few moments, the prophetess continued: "But to the king of Judah, who sent you to inquire of the Lord, thus shall you say to him, 'Thus says the Lord, the God of Israel: Regarding the words that you have heard, because your heart was penitent, and you humbled yourself before the Lord, when you heard how I spoke against this place and against its inhabitants, that they should become a desolation and a curse, and you have torn your clothes and wept before me, I also have heard you, declares the Lord. Therefore, behold, I will gather you to your fathers, and you shall be gathered to your grave in peace, and your eyes shall not see all the disaster that I will bring upon this place.' "

Asaiah's look of anger melted away. As long as his beloved king was not to suffer or be criticised, he did not concern himself with much else.

The others likewise appeared to have been placated by these words that seemed to herald decades of ongoing peace for the nation.

"Is that all you have to tell us?" asked Hilkiah.

"Yes," replied Huldah.

"Did you know that we were coming?" asked Ahikam, seeming intrigued by the idea.

"Yes," replied Huldah again. "Yahweh told me who would visit and why, and gave me the words I have spoken to you for the king."

They left the house and the group of children scattered again as the lords made their way back along the street. It was a jovial group that left their unfamiliar surroundings and made their way back to the splendour of King Josiah's palace. The threatening first half of Huldah's message seemed to have been forgotten in the comfort of the second half.

Shaphan the Secretary strode along the streets calmly, satisfied that the young king would be able to put his fears behind him. Huldah's message had shown that Josiah had nothing to worry about and no need to drag the nation into some paroxysm of repentance. Seeing his king humbling himself and tearing his clothes in such an excess of guilt had been almost embarrassing.

Life could return to normal, with the extra confidence of guaranteed peace.

But a hint of doubt crept into his mind as he thought of the last words of Huldah's message: "your eyes will not see all the disaster that I will bring on this place." He knew the king well enough to wonder whether he would feel that he had a responsibility to do his best to delay or even avoid that promised disaster. It was possible that Josiah would still take these threats a little too seriously.

He sighed: Josiah might still give the nation a big shakeup. Sometimes he seemed a little more religious than Shaphan could fully understand.

Nine

Passover Preparations

For the true story, see 2 Kings 23:21-23; 2 Chronicles 35:1-19.

The servant arranged the evening meal on an ornately carved table as a young couple in fine clothes waited patiently nearby.

"King Josiah has invited people from all over Israel and Judah to attend the Passover," said the man to his wife. His voice was deep and pleasant to listen to. "There will be thousands of visitors coming, Abigail – thousands! – and so now he wants to hear from anyone who is willing to welcome any of the visitors to stay in their home during the feast."

"How long will the feast last?"

"As I understand it, the Passover itself is just one evening, but the Feast of Unleavened Bread which immediately follows it lasts for seven days."

"Have you found out yet what the Feast of Unleavened Bread is all about?"

"Our house will need to be cleaned of leaven. All of it must go, and for the whole length of the feast we are only allowed to eat things without any yeast in them."

"That shouldn't be too hard, although it will be different from what we are used to."

"And how do we get the leaven back again afterwards, Abigail? Normally when you make bread, you just keep some of the dough to mix with the next batch, don't you? What happens when we get rid of all the yeast from the house?"

"Oh, it's not hard, Zaccai. We just mix some flour and water and wait for a few days. The leaven comes easily enough."

"That's good. I think we'll be learning a few new things with this feast."

The meal had now been attractively laid out and the servant withdrew. Zaccai and Abigail sat down and began to eat, still discussing the upcoming feast. Although there were only two of them, the room in which they sat was large and spacious. Zaccai was in his mid-twenties, quite tall, with a pleasant-looking face and a neat beard, while Abigail was a very attractive young woman a few years younger than he. They had been married for five years already, but no children had yet come of their union. It was a source of grief to both, and their new and growing love for the God of their fathers gave them somewhere to direct their requests for children.

Neither had known very much about Yahweh and his ways until Josiah began to push his nation towards the God who had saved his nation from Egypt. The feasts had not been kept since the reign of Hezekiah, and few knew anything about them. Indeed, there had been little in the temple to lead people to Yahweh. It held far more altars to other gods than reminders of Yahweh – until Josiah had begun his outstanding work. Now there was much more information available through prophets and priests, and Zaccai and Abigail found the worship of Yahweh unexpectedly attractive. It was a worship built on purity and a separation from evil – so different from the horrific worship of the many idols of Canaan that had taken such an important position in the life of the nation.

"Should we invite people to stay in our house, Zaccai? We have lots of room."

"Do we have any relatives we should invite first?"

"Most of my relatives live in Jerusalem, or near enough to easily take part in any of the celebrations each day, and I think most of yours are the same."

"Yes, though my mother has a few relatives from further south. We could ask them, but if they come at all they are more likely to stay with my parents anyway."

"You mean the ones who wouldn't come to Jerusalem even when King Josiah read the Book of the Law?"

"Yes, those are the ones. Really, it doesn't seem likely that they will come unless they've had a sudden change of heart."

"Probably not, but don't you think we should at least ask them?"

"I suppose so. It would be good for them to learn more about Yahweh. I'll talk to my father tomorrow."

Josiah had been king for 18 years when the Book of the Law was discovered. Armed with the extra knowledge it provided, he had ordered that the Passover feast be kept in Jerusalem. He had also made it clear that the invitation was extended to everyone in Judah, and even to those in Israel. As a result, the inhabitants of Jerusalem were being asked to give careful thought to providing accommodation for visitors.

Many of the inhabitants of Jerusalem had spent at least some of the long evenings of that rainy winter considering which of their relatives they could invite to stay with them or whether they should instead welcome completely unknown worshippers into their house.

Numerous letters had been sent to relatives and friends with invitations to join in the festivities in Jerusalem. The king's enthusiasm was catching, and the number of positive responses was astonishing. Some might be coming just to see what all the fuss was about, but they would find a city filled from end to end with excited worshippers.

Reports from areas outside Jerusalem were already showing that many who planned to come – particularly those from the areas of subjugated Israel – would not have any relatives or friends who could put them up in their houses. Where would they stay?

Zaccai visited his parents the following day, and his mother happily told him that her relatives would indeed be coming to the great feast and staying with them.

"It was quite a surprise to me," he told Abigail later in the day.

"Well, it is hard to resist Josiah's enthusiasm," she said, smiling. "After all, we couldn't!"

"It's amazing how much difference the reading of the Book of the Law made, too. So many of us now feel that we know a bit of what life should really be like."

"And prophets like Jeremiah are helping with that too. If people won't turn to Yahweh because of Josiah's encouragement, maybe they will turn to him through Jeremiah's warnings instead."

"Yes, he's a very serious young man, and his warnings are grave. I wonder if things really are as bad as he says."

"You've told me before that King Josiah believes him completely, and Huldah the prophetess agrees too, so why would you doubt him, Zaccai?"

"Oh, it's just hard to believe that things can really be so terribly bad when we have a good king and so many are turning away from idols to worship Yahweh."

"I haven't been obeying God's commands very well myself – I didn't even know them," argued Abigail. "And I know that my parents haven't either, nor my grandparents. It's hard to see how Yahweh could be pleased with us. We haven't been worshipping him properly for generations."

"That's true, but surely he is pleased that we are listening to him *now*? And I don't really think you have been too bad, my dear."

"If you were a king whose subjects had ignored him and his rules for months, didn't pay taxes, didn't answer questions, broke his rules, fought in other armies and generally did whatever they wanted, would you be happy? Then imagine that some of them started to pay *some* of their taxes – just every so often – would you be willing to forget all of their failures, the taxes they still owed and everything else? God is meant to be our king, and our failures have been going on for centuries, not just a few months or years."

"I suppose you are right, Abigail. I hadn't thought of it that way. But when I do so, I start to wonder whether there is any way that we can ever make peace with God after so much rebellion."

"I think all we can do is repent and try to do better from now on."

"You're probably right, and one of the ways we can do better is to offer lodgings to some people who come faithfully to Jerusalem to keep the feast."

"I would like that, Zaccai."

"Then I shall put our names on the king's register."

❦

As the time for the Passover feast drew closer, and the first hints of spring appeared in the city and on the surrounding hills, the magnitude of the task Josiah had taken on became clearer.

The king had sent messengers throughout the cities and villages of Judah and Israel, calling everyone to come to Jerusalem in time for the fourteenth day of the first month. "Don't be late!" was the king's urgent reminder; "We won't be able to wait." Thousands from all over the country gave their word to the king's messengers, and as the time approached, the numbers were tallied in Jerusalem.

One week before the feast, Shaphan the secretary saw the expected number of visitors and raised his eyebrows. He showed the numbers to Maaseiah, the governor of the city, and the response was little short of spectacular.

"What?" shouted Maaseiah. "You must have made a mistake with your adding. We can't possibly fit that many people in Jerusalem, however tightly we pack them in!"

"I don't think there's been any mistake in counting," replied Shaphan, quietly. "My chief of staff said that he checked the numbers five times because he couldn't believe them."

"I'm not surprised he couldn't believe them," said Maaseiah grimly, but calming down a little. "They must be impossible, surely?"

"Well, you can be sure that some people who planned to come will be sick and unable to come."

"Yes, and probably some who thought they were too sick to come have now recovered and are setting off as we speak."

"Actually, I've heard that some people have already set off, to make sure that they get a good position, whether in the city or outside on the hills."

Maaseiah put his hands to his head. "We have arranged as many billets as possible. Everyone with a room big enough to fit a person lying down has already been asked to fit two or three people in it. All of the squares are full of temporary sleeping quarters. We've even cleared all of the streets so that we can use them if we need to."

"Well, you may be surprised to hear it, but King Josiah was pleased when I told him the number."

"He's not doing the organisation."

"No, but he is paying for most of it."

"I suppose so. And I suppose that means he is very serious about it. Strange, really."

"Why, Maaseiah?"

"Well, it's already been a big few months, and calling everyone to Jerusalem again just seems a little bit over the top."

"Yahweh is important to the king, you know."

"Yes, I understand that, but wasn't the crowd that came to listen to the reading of the Book of the Law enough?"

"If these numbers are right, many more people will be coming for the Passover than came to hear the Book of the Law. But no, the king won't be satisfied until *everyone* is coming along *every year*. Just think how crowded your city will be then... and try to keep your mouth closed, Maaseiah – it doesn't look very statesmanlike."

Ten

Habakkuk's Complaints

For the true story, see the book of Habakkuk.

I stood on the wall of Lachish this morning and watched the sunrise. It was a beautiful sight: the star-filled sky gradually lightening from black to grey and the wispy clouds becoming fingers of pink, spreading across the sky, slowly turning to orange and then gold. Finally, the sun rose as a ball of fire, surging above the horizon and beginning its steady march across the sky.

Yet all the beauty of the sight could not distract me from the horror of last night. It was the culmination of all that I have been seeing is wrong with our nation. Josiah is a good king, yet the nation he rules is infested with evil. Maybe if he lived here in Lachish, the scenes that occur on a daily basis would not be seen – but he is in Jerusalem, and there is much that goes on behind his back, away from the capital, that he knows nothing about.

When he began his well-known attempts to lead his nation back to the worship of Yahweh, there was support for his aims. People joined him in his efforts. The eighteenth year of his reign was a time of joyful reform. Many from all over Judah and even the desolated places in Israel attended his reading of the Book of the Law. Even more attended that great Passover feast and I'm sure that Josiah considered it a watershed moment. Surely the direction of the nation had changed!

But it wasn't long before the enthusiasm of the people for godliness began to wane, and as a nation, we soon drifted back to our old ways. Maybe things are even worse. Josiah can enforce some things all over the country, and often appearances are kept up to satisfy him, but his influence outside of Jerusalem is limited. So we have a good king, but an evil nation.

I have been praying fervently about this, but nothing improves.

Last night was just another example of how bad things are. I work as a watchman for the city[14] and had just come on duty when the first incident happened.

There were three men sitting in the market area who were obviously drunk. Another man went to walk past nearby and the three drunken men began to abuse him. From what they all said, I guessed that the fourth man was a neighbour of one of the three and that there was no love lost between them. Sneers and curses began to flow freely, and soon the three drunks attacked the lone man and beat him up. Before long he was lying senseless on the ground and the three were back to their drinking. It had all happened too quickly for me to go and interfere, and I wasn't sure that I should be leaving my post anyway.

---

[14] We do not know for sure what Habakkuk did as a job, however, after his second complaint, he talks about going to stand on his watch post on the tower (Habakkuk 2:1).

As darkness fell I kept a bit of an eye on the group and noticed that they kept kicking their victim from time to time and that he didn't seem to be recovering consciousness. After a while, I told one of my mates who was on duty with me that I was going to check on something, and climbed down the steps into the market area. Crossing to the drunken trio, I asked them about the man they had attacked. One laughingly told me that he was still asleep and that maybe the sleep would teach him some manners. The others laughed uproariously as if he had told a hilarious joke, and one took the opportunity to kick the fallen man once more.

"Stop it!" I said, angrily.

They looked at me in surprise and even anger, but drew back when they saw that I was a member of the watch, and armed.

I knelt down beside the victim in the gloom and saw that the back of his head had been crushed and a rock lay near his head. Presumably as he lay unconscious, one of them had found the rock nearby and idly dropped it on his head, killing him.

"You've murdered him," I said, a little shocked.

"Oh, it was just what he deserved," one answered.

"Everyone has to die sometime," laughed another.

"Better him than me," mumbled the third.

There was nothing I could do, so I climbed back to the top of the wall and found the captain of the guard. I reported what had happened and that I was willing to be a witness against these men for what I had seen of the attack.

"Don't worry about it, Habakkuk. I'll organise for the body to be collected, but it's not likely to come to court.

Drunken brawls take people off every day, and as often as not, the people who die deserve it."

"But sir," I protested, "these men verbally abused a man, then attacked him, three against one. And while he was unconscious, one of them killed him. That's not a drunken brawl, it's most likely to be murder!"

"Look, we don't have time to settle every dispute in the city, or to protect fools who get themselves in trouble. This isn't Jerusalem, you know."

I argued unsuccessfully for a while before being told to shut up and get back to my post.

I might not have been so upset if this had been an isolated incident, but I had witnessed or heard of many such over the past two or three years. It had become quite common, and nobody was willing to do anything about it. Whenever I complained to my captain or to the judges, I was either ignored or shouted down.

As it turned out, that was just the first incident for the night. It wasn't much later that I heard screams from below. They were muffled and sounded as if they came from inside one of the houses next to the market. A man's shouts mingled with the screams – probably one of the domestic arguments that are common in that area. Once again I wondered: what should I do? I had a job to do and I couldn't be constantly leaving the wall to settle minor disputes. As I hesitated, the shouting and screaming continued, growing even louder.

Suddenly, a door opened and a woman burst out into the square, followed at a run by a man carrying a heavy stick. I won't report their words; suffice it to say that they were threatening, blasphemous and altogether vile. There wasn't much light down there in the square, but I hurried down to see if I could help. After the earlier death, I didn't want another on my watch. I drew my sword and quickly grabbed a torch that hung against the wall before running towards the sounds. By the time I arrived, the man had caught the woman and thrown her to the ground where she lay helpless as he hit at her with his stick. The darkness probably saved her, but I also shouted to distract him and struck at his stick with my sword as he raised it again to strike.

"Stop it!" I commanded once more.

I won't go into all the details of that encounter either. My attack made the man drop his cudgel and he was very angry about that. He was also angry that I had interrupted him in the middle of his legitimate business: beating his wife.

The long and the short of it was that, when I helped his wife to her feet and asked her if she needed any help or protection, she spat in my face.

What could I do? They walked off together and I left them to settle their dispute in their own way – but how could that ever be right? *That* incident I didn't bother reporting to my boss.

The night wore on and I was left to watch over the wall in the moonless blackness that makes the job of a watchmen particularly stressful. During such nights, you avoid turning to look back into the city because the slightest light of a fire will steal away your hard-earned night vision, leaving you completely blind.

In those conditions, even with night vision, a horde of heavily armed warriors could easily skulk in the shadows without ever being seen. And last night there was a gentle breeze blowing that made enough noise to mask any muffled sounds that a careful horde might make. Yes, on those nights you see shadows moving, and imagine all sorts of terrifying threats.

At times like that, it is my faith in God that keeps me strong, but my faith has been shaken a little by the senseless evil that I see so much of in the city. My prayers have long been full of entreaties to God asking him to deal with the iniquity and violence that are so prevalent.

Last night, I was edgy and worried.

By the end of the second watch of the night I was longing for my replacement to come, as I was due to have a rest during the third watch. I waited and waited, then finally made my way to the command room. As I entered, the captain looked up at me and snarled, "What do you want?"

Now the captain and I generally get on alright, although he doesn't like my attitudes or my beliefs, but at that point he was obviously angry.

"Where is my replacement?" I asked.

"There," he said, pointing to a huddled pile of clothes that lay behind a table a small distance from him.

"What happened?"

"He tried to blackmail me. Me! The captain of the guard!"

"And what did you do?"

"I ran him through with my sword."

"Was that necessary? Did he attack you?"

"No. But he deserved what he got. Threatening me!"

So I didn't get my break. Instead, I had to explain to my boss why I didn't like what he had done. I kept very alert while I did so and didn't turn my back on him for an instant. Then I went back on watch.

And there you have it. Three incidents of unjustified violence in a night, and an undercurrent of evil that filled me with horror.

By the time sunrise came, I was tired and very upset, desperate to find somewhere to hide so that I could complain to God. As soon as I was relieved, I went home and began to pray:

> "O Lord, how long shall I cry for help,
>> and you will not hear?
>> Or cry to you "Violence!"
>> and you will not save?
>> Why do you make me see iniquity,
>> and why do you idly look at wrong?
>> Destruction and violence are before me;
>>> strife and contention arise.
>>> So the law is paralysed,
>> and justice never goes forth.
>> For the wicked surround the righteous;
>> so justice goes forth perverted."[15]

I'm afraid that all of my worry and discontent forced their way into the prayer and it ended up nothing more than a complaint about how God runs the world. After all, he told us in the Book of the Law that evil people would be punished, yet here the city was filled with evil – evil people who prospered.

I didn't really expect God to answer me when I complained to him, but he did.

---

[15] Habakkuk 1:2-4

"Look among the nations, and see;" he said,
"wonder and be astounded.
For I am doing a work in your days
that you would not believe if told.
For behold, I am raising up the Chaldeans,
that bitter and hasty nation,
who march through the breadth of the earth,
to seize dwellings not their own.
They are dreaded and fearsome;
their justice and dignity go forth from themselves.
Their horses are swifter than leopards,
more fierce than the evening wolves;
their horsemen press proudly on.
Their horsemen come from afar;
they fly like an eagle swift to devour.
They all come for violence,
all their faces forward.
They gather captives like sand.
At kings they scoff,
and at rulers they laugh.
They laugh at every fortress,
for they pile up earth and take it.
Then they sweep by like the wind and go on,
guilty men, whose own might is their god!"[16]

His words left me speechless. I couldn't believe that I was really understanding them. Was God really saying that he was going to send the *Chaldeans* to attack and punish his people for the evils I was complaining about? Surely that was like sending an assassin to punish a petty thief or using a sledgehammer to squash a moth!

---

[16] Habakkuk 1:5-11

I decided that I would not be hasty, but must consider God's answer carefully to make sure that I really understood it.   I even began to wonder whether perhaps I don't understand God as well as I've always thought I do.

Eleven

Fingers of Fear

For the true story, see Daniel 5.

Look, I confess that my hands are a little pudgy – and my legs too, to be honest – but nothing like Belshazzar. He is pudginess personified. Yet those pudgy knees were knocking together quite firmly earlier this evening, despite the fact that all of him was wobbling with fear.

And, yes, I must confess that as well – I was also a little scared, and may have been shaking in my boots as well. Ha-ha-ha! But I was a bit tipsy at the time, since we were in the middle of a wonderful party. Now, of course, I'm completely sober – because of that hand.

Of course, Belshazzar isn't really the king, and everyone knows why, although we never talk about it, and we all call him "king". After all, you can't say anything against a king who is... but never mind. I can't say that we don't talk about it and then talk about it, can I?

Back to the point.

The party started well. In fact it was just the sort of party that we all like: the sort of party that makes a king popular. I was pleased as punch to be invited, although I wasn't really surprised. One thousand lords were invited and, of course, I would always be included in a net cast that widely! One thousand? Why, I would be in the top hundred, perhaps. Yes, I'm sure I would – the top hundred, to be sure. After all, wasn't I invited to his investiture when he was announced king? And haven't I attended many – well, at least several – of his parties over the years since?

No-one could dispute the fact that I move in the upper echelons of Babylonian society. And if Urukh or Nergal ever try to tell you about that time when I was not invited to that celebration, there was a perfectly simple explanation, because... Oh, never mind – they are as narrow minded and self-seeking as their fathers were. I shouldn't even acknowledge their snide remarks!

This is just to be a simple account of what happened tonight, just in case it really was important. And maybe by tomorrow I won't remember what happened – it wouldn't be the first time.

Now let me get the order right. I'm a bit fuzzy on the details, although I clearly remember being led to my seat by a servant and being greeted and welcomed by no less a person than Muranu, who is one of Belshazzar's relatives! He spent *several* minutes talking to us, and I noticed Urukh watching, green with envy, from where he sat at a table that was definitely lower than ours – and further from the king.

I was revelling in it until I noticed Nergal looking at me with a supercilious smirk – you've probably seen it before whenever he is advanced in any way. There was that last celebration in the Esagila when he was put in an honoured position – accidentally, I think. I firmly believe that the steward mixed him up with someone else when he offered him that special wine. As if he deserves to be honoured in such a way, when people like me are treated with little respect, despite my constant attention to the worship of all of our gods. After all, who was it who began the habit – a habit that everyone now follows – of wearing a square of coloured material on the feast days or when the priests tell us that we should be remembering particular gods? Wasn't it me? And yes, I know that others have claimed the idea, but they only ever used ragged shreds of material, and they only acknowledged a few gods on whom they had set their preference. *I* was the one who had the original thought of hemming the material and dutifully acknowledging all of our gods with consistently shaped and trimmed clouts, not just a few scraps.

Now, almost everyone follows my example. Why, even at tonight's feast, a day when there was no feast for any particular god, some people were still wearing a patch of orange from yesterday's religious feast. I am humbly, but justly, proud of my success in this. Even some of the priests have told me that they are pleased with this acknowledgement of the gods.

And that brings me back to the subject of tonight's feast. I don't seem to be able to concentrate on one subject. Maybe I'm not as sober as I thought, despite that scare a while ago. Just let me go back to the beginning so that I can get my thoughts in order.

Belshazzar started the feast with food, but it wasn't long before there was a lot of wine flowing too. Belshazzar is rather proud of his ability to put away litres of wine without becoming, ah, "tired and emotional." I have to admit that he puts me to shame – it's a real gift he has.

He was seated at his special table, raised above the floor level of the banquet hall. His chair is not only beautifully carved, but also rather heavily reinforced, so he has two slaves standing behind him all the time, ready to move the chair whenever he needs them to.

Many of his wives were there too, trying to look regal and relaxed, while covertly jockeying for position with the king. Most of the time, though, he seems to be more interested in his concubines anyway – and some of *them* will dress up in amazing ways to get his attention.

So that was the front table: the king and his women.

Then, the nearest tables contained the king's closest advisors and friends, hanging on his every word and trying to emulate his skill for tolerating strong drink. No advisor will ever get far with the king if he can't carry his wine well.

There were also some of the religious elite. They're always good with wine, and good with the women too – although they have to be careful near the king's women. Their religious importance won't save them if the king suspects anything.

None of this will be new to anyone. There was nothing unusual in anything that happened in the earlier parts of the feast. Everything followed the established practices. That's why I'm writing it down: all of this has happened before, but without the aftermath.

The food was exquisite, brought in on large platters by beautiful slaves, and some of the exotic dishes there would have cost me a month's income – and I'm not poor!

Wine flowed freely, and gradually the room got noisier and everyone was happy. Even my wife was enjoying herself for once, although she wasn't pleased with the way she said I looked at one of the slave-girls; but then, she's always been a bit like that. And anyway, it was only a slave-girl!

There were jugglers too, and I tried to imitate one of them – and I was doing very well too, until my wife knocked my elbow and made me drop the goblets I was juggling. Everybody on the next table had been cheering me, before she interfered.

Yes, everything about the party was going well, but nothing unusual was happening until the king suddenly had an idea. He was holding a golden goblet at the time, and I just happened to be watching him as he looked at it and ran his finger around the rim. He was talking to his chief wife at the time and looking a bit bored. Sometimes she treats him more like a child than her king – lecturing him, you might say – and he doesn't like it.

Suddenly he threw the priceless goblet down on the floor and called his steward.

"I'm bored with these goblets," he cried. "Don't we have some different ones that we can use? Ones from some far distant country that we of Babylon have conquered?"

The steward looked a bit nonplussed and then said, "I'll go and see what I can find, sire."

He hurried out and Belshazzar waited.

One of his closest friends, Zikar-sin, had obviously been watching and heard what was said, for he called across to the king, "Why not get some of the golden cups that were taken from one of the temples we have conquered? Drink yourself drunk out of cups dedicated to a failed god! Show everyone that a king of Babylon is greater than any of these foreign gods."

Belshazzar still looked completely sober, but his laugh was a little too loud; a little too shrill.

"Ah-huh," he said, gurgling with laughter. "Yes, I've wanted to do that for years with the cups from the temple of that god in Jerusalem. Some people treat him as so important, but he's just another failed god like all the rest of them."

Zikar-sin looked a little uncomfortable as he replied, "Are you sure, sire? I've heard some things about that god that make me wonder – at least when I'm sober."

"You're just a coward, Zikar-sin," said the king, and banged on the table with a silver tankard until the under-steward came.

"Go and tell... the steward, whatever his name is, that I want all of the cups from the temple of Yahweh in Jerusalem," said Belshazzar. "We're going to have fun with them."

"Yes, sire. Anything you say, sire."

He hurried off and Belshazzar drank another tankard of wine to stave off his thirst while he waited.

It really wasn't long, but Belshazzar was getting a bit edgy by the time the steward returned with five men, each carrying a wooden box. He signalled to one of the men, who opened his box and passed the king several heavy-looking cups. They were obviously made of gold, and Belshazzar studied them one by one.

"Are these from the temple of Yahweh?" he asked.

"Yes, sire."

"Were they used in worship of Yahweh?"

"I believe so, sire. They have been sitting in the treasury ever since they arrived. They have never been used for anything in Babylon."

"Well, now they will be. And much better things than they were used for in Jerusalem." Belshazzar leaned forward and spat in one of the cups. "Hah-hah," he said, emptying the cup on the floor. "They're not very clean! Is this all there are?"

"No, there are thousands of them, my lord."

"Good." He waved an unsteady hand around the room. "Clean up enough cups for everyone here to have one."

"Everyone, sir?" asked the steward, looking around the crowded room at the throng that had fallen strangely silent.

"Yes, everyone."

"Very well, sire."

The cups were duly cleaned, and soon about 50 men were distributing the golden cups amongst us. I took the cup I was offered and looked at it carefully. I, too, had heard some rumours about the god of Israel, and if I had been sober, maybe I would have thought twice before taking it. But I wasn't sober – not completely – and I quickly had the cup filled with wine.

Nothing could go wrong. I knew that.

ҀҎ

The golden cup I'd been given felt cool and heavy in my hand. Into its otherwise silky-smooth surface were etched strange pictures of what looked like humans with wings and several faces. There was writing too, but it was in a script that I couldn't recognise – I guess that it must have been Hebrew. From all I had heard about Yahweh, these cups wouldn't have been used in a feast like this one before. Belshazzar himself had a particularly large cup, and it was being refilled often. I didn't notice it at the time, but in thinking back now, I can see that his attitude showed no respect towards the cup or thought for its origin. In fact, some of the things he did were obviously specifically intended to belittle the temple it came from.

By that time, the feast had reached a stage where quite a few of us were a little worse for wear. Voices were growing loud and arguments were springing up all around the enormous banqueting hall. One of the king's wives had to be told firmly to be quiet after her alternating laughter and tears became too much for the king to tolerate. Two concubines were spitting at each other and had to be separated. Other concubines were doing all they could to get the king (and everyone else) to notice them. No surprise really – isn't that what they're there for? Everyone knows that, and I believe they even teach them such things in the harem.

All that I'm trying to say here is that, even at that stage, nothing unusual was happening – except that those golden cups were being used in ways they had never been used before.

Then came the incident that seemed to spark the trouble.

Belshazzar seemed to feel some deep-seated inner need to sneer at Yahweh, the god of Israel. The banquet hall has images of many of our gods around the perimeter, and the king's massive chair is covered with carvings of gods as well. He often mentions them in his conversation, and his stories are littered with how the various gods have helped him and his family.

On this occasion, though, he decided to go a bit further, and called the steward in again. Incidentally, I'm glad I don't have his job! Belshazzar wanted some more statues and idols brought in, and he kept laughing as he gave the man his instructions.

Since I was beginning to feel a little sleepy, I was happy to sit back and quietly watch what was going on. I was warm and relaxed, half-reclining with my golden cup resting on my tummy, sipping a little wine from time to time. It would have been an ideal end to my memories of the feast if only my wife hadn't seen that I was comfortable and started hectoring me. She can't bear to see me happy, and likes to take advantage of me when I'm not myself and can't argue with her.

Well, it woke me up enough to be able to pointedly ignore her, watching the king's table instead, where the steward was directing some of his men as they laid out beautiful and elegant statues of various gods around Belshazzar. From small, magnificently crafted golden statuettes to squat, roughly carved lumps of stone, the gods of Babylon were on show, and Belshazzar had encouraged us all to honour them.

So I touched my forehead as we do and inclined my head in acknowledgement of the gods. Looking down made me notice that beautiful golden cup again, and I took a quick swig before looking up again. Belshazzar was pushing back his chair and standing up slowly with the help of his attendants.

He was a little shaky on his feet as he began to speak, "Our gods have blesshed us wonder... wonder-fully." He carries his wine well, but there are limits!

"Ea made the world. 'E made it and makes the grants to plough so that we... ah, the plants to grow so that we have food to eat..." He hesitated a little as he began to sway and had to grab at his chair. His balance restored, he smiled, held up his goblet and continued, "And wine to drink, as well. Wine and worship are good. Wine and worship and women... and wealth." He might have continued with his alliteration had not he lost his balance again and reached desperately for the back of his chair, dropping the goblet as he did so. Wine sprayed over one of his concubines who was sitting near him on the floor for some reason I couldn't work out. I suppose she was drunk.

Belshazzar staggered around for a few moments before finding his balance again. He was laughing as he lurched about, and the laughter spread through the hall amongst those who were still able to join in.

"Wine and women," he repeated, "...and worship. Banquets, too. Of course, the great Nergal gives us hangovers, and the only solution is more wine, more women and more worship." Belshazzar giggled and called for a new goblet.

He continued with a rambling verbal dissertation on the glories of our gods. By the time he finished, many of those in the hall were completely inebriated, and I wasn't much better myself. But I was awake, so I saw what happened next.

The next part of Belshazzar's speech had obviously been part of his plan from the beginning. Having finished his comments on our gods, he began an attack on Yahweh, the god of Judah. Based on the strange things that have happened since, I think it is best not to repeat what he said.

I may still be drunk, but I can tell you, I'm worried.

Well, Belshazzar was doing his drunken best to show the superiority of our gods over Yahweh when suddenly the fingers of a human hand appeared.

Disembodied fingers.

Moving purposefully, they approached the wall in the full light of the candlestick.

Then they started to write on the plaster of the wall. I saw them – and so did Belshazzar.

When I'm in a comfortable haze of alcohol, I don't get upset easily, but I remember blinking several times before my brain could accept what my eyes were seeing.

Belshazzar stopped talking immediately, and he was blinking too. Then he started to shake. His face had been its usual uneven reddish hue, but suddenly it was white, or maybe even a pale greyish-green. He tried speaking again, but he couldn't.

He couldn't take his eyes off those fingers as they etched strange symbols into the wall of his palace. Then his legs gave way and he collapsed into his chair.

"What's going on?" he cried, but his voice was shrill and cracked. "Where are those fingers from? Who's playing a trick on me?"

He tried to stand again, but he couldn't. Instead, he watched transfixed as those fingers gouged with irresistible force into the brightly-coloured surface of his wall, leaving behind strange symbols in the stark white of the plaster.

It really didn't take long, and when they had finished writing, the fingers disappeared.

After a few moments, Belshazzar regained some of his composure and demanded loudly, "Bring in the enchanters, the Chaldeans, and the astrologers!" The chief of the army left immediately, and it wasn't long before a crowd of these experts stood around the king's table, staring in amazement at the writing on the wall.

"Whoever reads this writing, and shows me its interpretation, will be clothed with purple," Belshazzar announced. "And he'll have a chain of gold around his neck and shall be the third ruler in the kingdom."

It was a tempting offer, and the wise men were all eager to help the king – or at least, to gain the reward! But none of them could read the strange symbols on the wall, let alone interpret what they meant. If possible, Belshazzar looked even more worried than before. I'm not sure, but I think that he already suspected that these events had been sparked by his ridiculing of Yahweh, the god of Israel.

As the last of the wise men excused himself, the queen[17] came in. Nobody else would have had the confidence to come in uninvited – and nobody else would have dared to speak to the king as she did. Her words were polite, but she spoke as if to a child. Maybe I'm a bit sensitive because of the

---

[17] We don't know exactly who "the queen" is. The account states that Belshazzar's wives and concubines were included in the feast, yet the queen enters later. Her words also suggest that she knew more of Daniel's background than Belshazzar did, which suggests that she was probably older. She may have been his mother or even his grandmother. In fact, some translations translate this as "queen mother" or something similar.

way my wife speaks to me, but she certainly sounded confident, and Belshazzar looked helpless.

The queen declared, "O king, live forever! Don't be alarmed. You don't need to be so pale, either, because there is a man in your kingdom in whom is the spirit of the holy gods." She went on to explain that this man, called Daniel, was able to explain riddles and solve problems that no-one else could. The name was familiar to me; he was one of the old fuddy-duddies who had worked for Nebuchadnezzar back in the days when everyone seemed to take everything far too seriously. I got the feeling that all that mattered to them was discipline. We have far more fun now – though I must admit that nobody seemed to be having fun tonight once that hand appeared!

Anyway, Belshazzar took her advice and had Daniel called into the banquet hall.

I have to say that this Daniel is an amazing old man. He must be in his 80s or 90s and obviously doesn't attend late-night parties very often. Yet he stood straight and strong before the wobbling mass of fear that was Belshazzar, and showed that he wasn't looking pleased with what he saw. The king went through a grand introduction, spelling out the terms of his generous offer of fame and wealth, but Daniel wasn't impressed.

He said to the king, "You can keep your gifts for yourself, and give your rewards to someone else. But I will read the writing to the king and make known its interpretation."

Daniel then showed his extra-serious attitude by lecturing the king about how Yahweh – he called him "the Most High God", as a putdown to our gods – had worked hard to teach King Nebuchadnezzar his requirements, and claiming that Belshazzar should have learned from that. He condemned Belshazzar for honouring gods of gold and silver, wood and stone, but failing to honour the god who had given him life. Oh, it was a stinging lecture, and I wondered if Belshazzar would have the old man hung from the rafters, but he was still too afraid.

Then Daniel read the words from the wall – something about counting and weights and stuff. He interpreted them too – but his interpretation was even more damning than his earlier words! Daniel said that it meant that Belshazzar was not good enough and that Yahweh had brought his kingdom to an end! Imagine that: the defeated local god of a subject nation like Judah claiming that he could interfere in the kingdom of Babylon!

But then again, maybe he can. Who sent those fingers?

I don't know: could that god really bring Belshazzar's kingdom to an end? And does that mean that the glorious kingdom of Babylon with all of its splendour is finished? Could that really happen? Won't Babylon go on forever?

As I have been writing this account, I have heard noises spreading through the city. Worrying noises. Coming nearer. Something is afoot, I'm sure, but I'm too afraid to go out and look.

Anyway, to wrap up, Belshazzar saw to it that Daniel was clothed with purple and a chain of gold was put around his neck, as promised. The man endured it, but I thought he looked as if he would prefer to go back to bed!

Belshazzar also made a proclamation that Daniel should be the third ruler in the kingdom. I wouldn't have minded that myself – but then, if Daniel's interpretation is right, the kingdom is finished, so maybe it's a poisonous cup.

Now I can hear noises right outside the house. Men shouting; women screaming; the clash of weapons. Do I dare to go outside – or should I try to hide?

Part Two: New Testament

Twelve

Anna

For the true story, see Luke 2:36-38. Verses 22-35 also provide more background.

Are you waiting for the redemption of Jerusalem?

If you are, then I have something to tell you!

A baby boy was born in Bethlehem about six weeks ago, and this little baby is special. Very special.

He will bring redemption to Jerusalem. Imagine that! No more slavery; no more Roman domination – and no more domination by sin either. That's what this boy will bring. I can't wait for him to grow up – but I probably won't live that long.

Abraham was promised the land of Israel for himself and for his descendants forever. This child will fulfil that promise too.

I have waited many years for what happened today. And now, God has shown me his salvation.

Maybe you are wondering why you should listen to an old woman like me. Of course, you don't have to, but I hope that you will. I'm telling the truth, and it's important.

My past life is nothing special, except that I have lived for quite a long time and seen God's hand at work. You see, when I was a young girl, life seemed "normal". But as I grew older, I realised that I had grown up in a time of important international change. Often, we don't seem to recognise the importance of events until later – but today I recognised immediately just how important the child I met will be.

I've been told that Rome changed from a republic into an empire during my lifetime. All I know is that my country was once independent, but now is part of the Roman empire. I don't quite understand how having Rome fighting civil wars and putting down rebellions everywhere could result in Rome taking over so many more nations, but that's how it worked.

When I was young, I lived in the north of Israel in the area of Galilee and looked forward to marriage – as most young girls do. My parents' friends had a son who caught my eye; a handsome young man he was, and godly and courageous as well. Apparently I caught his eye too. Before I turned 19, I was married and very happy to be so.

Israel – or Judea as it was called – was fractured, but not completely helpless. The Samaritans were a problem in the middle of the country. They knew very little about Israel's religion, but thought that they knew a lot. The nations around us were a constant source of trouble too, although Syria in the north was weak enough that we had started to expand into some of their territory and take over some of their cities. Living where we did was safer than it had been when my parents were young.

But then Pompey came. First he went to Syria and threw his weight around there. The kingdom of the Seleucids in

Syria had been around since just after the reign of Alexander the Great. I'm told that it was falling apart by the time I was born, and Pompey merely finished it off. He turned it into a Roman province and ordered Judea to return the cities we had taken from Syria.

Pompey also created the league which he called "The Decapolis" – ten cities in Galilee and further north that were to be autonomous, but protected by the Roman legions of the province of Syria. More than half of those cities were under our control, so these demands were unwelcome and significant.

What can a small country do when the Roman Empire gives it orders? As you might expect, our leaders gave in. Mostly. But they also toyed with thoughts of rebellion.

Even before Pompey travelled south, living in Galilee had become quite dangerous, and it was obvious that things were going to get worse.

So, we decided to move to Jerusalem. My husband, Samuel, wanted to be able to defend God's temple if necessary.

Then, Pompey arrived in Jericho and demanded that Jerusalem be handed over. Aristobulus, our king, promised to give him Jerusalem and money, as long as he could still remain king. Pompey sent his representative to receive the money and the city, but the soldiers refused to let him in.

It was a very confused situation. Pompey took Aristobulus prisoner, then, while the soldiers defending the city were busy getting all upset about that, some of the people went and opened the gates.

In poured the Roman soldiers, and the defenders quickly withdrew to the temple, which had been heavily fortified to withstand an earlier attack.

Samuel was with them, while I was busy buying food in the market, blissfully ignorant of the terrifying events unfolding elsewhere in the city.

My first hint that the Romans were inside the city came when I heard screams from a nearby market stall and saw a group of soldiers coming toward me. Their swords were unsheathed, and they were obviously on edge. Men and women alike were scrambling to get out of their way, and any who were too slow were pushed out of the way with shields or struck down with swords. I was able to get out of their way without injury, but only just. No-one tried to fight, so there weren't many casualties. The soldiers were looking for organised resistance – they weren't interested in a crowd of unarmed people buying vegetables.

But many of us were worried about what they would do when they did find organised resistance – as we knew they would. We had husbands, fathers and other relatives who we knew would not allow the Romans to take over all of the city without resistance: the temple would never be handed over as long as dedicated men remained alive to defend it.

Several other groups of soldiers were gradually working their way through other parts of the market, but there was still no resistance and only a few had suffered for being too slow to get out of the way.

Meanwhile, I was frantic. What had happened to Samuel? I knew him well enough to be sure that if there was any organised defence of the temple, he would be part of it.

My husband was a godly man, and the temple was more important to him than life itself. By that time, we had been married for seven years – seven years of happiness. But Rome's insatiable desire for power had threatened our happiness by threatening the temple of God.

There was no way to get news without going to the temple myself, so I started to make my way there. Before the temple was even in sight, though, I saw a line of Roman soldiers forming a barrier, their spears and swords poised. Anyone who walked near was accosted by other soldiers who stood nearby, so I quickly turned around and walked away. I made my way around towards a different part of temple, but once again, a cordon of soldiers aggressively barred my way.

After trying a couple more places, I gave up and returned to the house in which we were staying. The city was swarming with Roman soldiers, and I passed many on the way. Most were not interested in a lone woman walking quietly through the streets, carrying a basket of vegetables and avoiding eye contact. But one was looking for trouble.

"A sweet young lady with a basket of food," he said in rough Greek. "Trying to smuggle it into the temple, no doubt. Helping the rebels, eh, miss?"

I quickly weighed up the risks and decided that getting some information was more important. But I had to be careful – my Greek was no better than his.

"I didn't know that there were any rebels, sir." I used a sweet voice, but not too sweet.

"There are always rebels among you Jews," he replied. "Women, too," he added, suspiciously.

"But you mentioned the temple, sir. I was there just this morning and there was no problem then."

"A whole bunch of rebels has taken over the temple and they're fighting us. Maybe one of them is your father – or your husband." He still sounded suspicious, and I didn't like the look in his eyes.

"I don't know of any rebels, sir," I answered, then decided to risk one question. "How will you fight them?"

"That will be up to Pompey the Great," he replied loftily, "but it's been suggested that we build a wall all around the temple and then...."

An officer approached as he spoke, and said something to him in another language – I suppose it must have been Latin. He was obviously warning the soldier not to talk too much about the army's plans. From the way they both looked at me, I decided to go before I got into trouble.

I turned and hurried away – just in time, I think.

Back at our lodgings, nobody knew exactly what was happening. That the Romans had taken control of Jerusalem was clear, but it seemed that the temple was not included.

From the noise that I heard late in the afternoon, I guess that the Romans attacked the temple several times before dark but were driven back.

Samuel didn't come home that night. I hoped and prayed that he was alright, and that God would keep him safe while he was defending God's temple.

Not knowing what was happening was the heaviest burden to bear. I knew that Samuel was willing to die defending the temple, but oh, how I hoped that he would not need to do so! I loved God as much then as I do now, but I loved Samuel too. Would I be able to keep them both?

As I lay awake alone that night, I remembered how the Roman soldier had suggested that women might help the rebels. Maybe I could help Samuel somehow. Tomorrow might show me the way.

☙

I couldn't sleep that night. Samuel, my husband, must be defending the temple from the Romans. I prayed fervently that God would look after him. On several occasions during the night, I heard the sound of fighting from the direction of the temple and thought how frightening it must be to fight in the dark against an enemy you couldn't see.

Dawn came eventually, and that day the Romans began to build a wall around the temple area so that no-one could enter or leave its precincts.

I spent the day trying to find out if there was any way I could help the defenders in the temple. Almost everybody told me that the best way to help was to keep out of trouble, but it soon became clear to me that some were concerned about a shortage of food in the temple. Those arranging for its defence had expected the Romans to be kept at bay outside the city for a time. When the attackers had been allowed to enter the city without resistance, the planned stores of food for the defenders had not yet been completely ready.

Was there anything that I could do to help? I continued to ask – ignoring the answers in the negative, since they seemed to contradict the thoughtful looks with which some people answered me. Naturally, people were cautious, so none of my enquiries were made in the streets. Instead, I found myself in public buildings associated with the priests and Levites, but separated from the ordinary administration of Jerusalem. One such building provided accommodation for non-resident priests who visited Jerusalem briefly when they were on duty – a sort of guest house for priests. After I had asked many questions there about what I could do, I was called quietly into a small room and assured that my Samuel was safe within the temple area and fighting bravely. It was good to hear news of him, but it just strengthened my determination to do something to help him and the defence of the temple of Yahweh. I wondered how they knew.

The Romans were in control of the city but frustrated by the fact that they did not control the temple. They were actively looking for anybody who might be working against them. They were also building their wall around the temple area very quickly indeed, providing themselves with good defensive positions, but also a place from which they could launch more substantial attacks. I feared for my Samuel and his colleagues who lay hidden in the temple, resisting the might of Rome and Pompey the Great.

The next day, as I approached the priests' guest house once again with my basket of food, I heard shouting before I could see the building itself. As I rounded the last corner, I saw a line of alert Roman soldiers spread across the open area in front of the building, while smoke poured out of the window nearest me. A few men lay, unmoving, on the ground near the cordon of soldiers. I was young and had never before seen anything like that, so I stood still and watched in open-mouthed shock. The fire seemed to be spreading inside the building, and from time to time, men dashed outside to escape the flames, only to be struck down by the waiting soldiers.

It was horrible to watch, but I could not tear my eyes away until two men came quietly around the corner behind me.

"Don't move, young lady. Stay just where you are – between us and the Romans," said the first.

"Alright," I said, "but why?"

"You're Samuel's wife, aren't you?" asked the second man, looking at me closely. I nodded. "You were asking for some way to help our defence. Well, this is it. Jacob and I are going to wait for a time when as many of the Romans as possible are distracted, and then we are going to attack them and kill as many as we can before they kill us."

It sounded a shocking thing to do, but how would I know what was best?

I turned back towards the priests' guest house and for a few minutes I stood silently watching, acutely aware of the two men crouching behind me, terrified that at any moment they might make a dash from behind me and throw away their lives in a fruitless attack on alert and well-armed soldiers. Instead, on the other side of the guest house I saw three men suddenly appear from behind another building and run silently towards the cordon of Roman soldiers, most of whom were facing towards the guest house at that moment. Knives were in the men's hands and they moved with great speed.

"Behind!" shouted a Roman soldier standing near me who was facing the attackers.

Immediately, every soldier who wasn't directly occupied with action in front of him turned around, weapons poised. The three brave Jews continued their attack, but now they were running towards a wall of swords and spears held by well-trained men who were not afraid to kill.

Within moments, it was over. Three Jews were dead and no Romans had even been hurt.

I heard an angry hiss from behind, "Let's go 'n' get 'em!"

Without thinking, I put my hand across in front of them and said quietly but urgently, "No, wait!"

Maybe it was just an accident of perfect timing, or maybe God was caring for those two men. Whatever the reason, the movement behind me stopped instantly. The Roman soldiers didn't seem to be paying much attention to me, so I turned around and said fiercely to the two men behind me, "How many will you kill that way? None, from the look of it."

"You could be right, lady," said Jacob. "What do you think, Joseph?"

"I'm not afraid to die for God – but maybe this isn't the best way."

"If only you had been able to be inside the temple, then you could have helped with defending it," I said. "That would have been much more useful, wouldn't it?"

"I think you're right," said Joseph, putting his knife away under his tunic. He looked across at Jacob and continued, "And maybe it's not too late to do just that. I'd like to pay them back for that." He gestured past the building to where the three bodies now lay, with soldiers examining them.

That was the end of our conversation. The men walked calmly back around the corner and I never saw them again. But they had got me thinking. I had heard a few people now making guarded suggestions that it was possible to get in contact with the defenders in the temple, and now Jacob and Joseph had hinted that it might even be possible to join them.

How?

The Roman soldiers wouldn't let anyone in – of that I was sure. Maybe an attack from outside was being planned. How could I find out? I didn't want to join in the fighting, but I did want to do anything else that I could to help with the defence of God's temple. In particular, I wanted to help Samuel.

It was another week before I got any further with my investigations. The Roman attack on the priests' guest house had killed quite a few significant people in the resistance, and made those who remained more cautious.

Nevertheless, I persisted and finally met a man who confirmed my fears that the defenders were running short of some supplies. He also admitted, very carefully, that there were ways of communicating with the defenders, and that it might even be possible to get supplies to them.

This was the breakthrough I had been hoping for. Immediately I volunteered to collect the supplies he said were needed. I also dropped hints that if I could help with getting the supplies to the defenders, I was eager to do so. To be honest, I was hoping to find some way of meeting Samuel!

I started collecting provisions that would last: parched grain, dried fruit, dried fish, nuts and other things to sustain the defenders if the siege continued a long time. Collecting was not always easy, as Samuel and I had not been living in

Jerusalem long, so I didn't know many people. It wasn't long, though, before everyone got to know me as the woman who went around pestering people for food! But I'm getting ahead of myself – my first efforts at collecting were limited because I wasn't very confident that what I collected would actually reach the defenders.

Once I had collected an amount that I thought would be a good test of what could be done, I made several trips and delivered it all to the building I had been instructed to visit. It was outside the new Roman wall, but still quite close to the temple. When I delivered the last of the provisions, I was led down into a large, mostly empty cellar to meet a group of men who looked as if they were probably all priests.

"Welcome, Anna, wife of Samuel," said their leader, whom I recognised as a priest from the temple. "Thank you for your work in helping our brave defenders of God's temple. We will do our best to get the food to them, but it is best if we don't tell you how. All we can say is that there are... ways into the temple that few know about. We have already used them for delivering messages and suchlike, but now we need to see if we can use them to deliver much larger amounts – enough food to stop thousands of our men from starving.

"If anyone asks you about this building or what you have been doing, try to hide as much as you can. If the Romans hear that we are bringing large amounts of food to a place near the temple, it won't take them long to figure out why."

I left and went to our home, and that night I spent a long time in prayer, asking for God's blessing on our efforts. The next day, I returned to the building and was told that the food had been transferred to the temple area without any problems. Could I please continue to collect the food that our gallant soldiers needed? Larger amounts would be needed.

I was eager to do so, but how long would it be before the Romans noticed what I was doing?

Once that first transfer had been successful, I began to collect food in earnest. Nobody could tell me exactly how many men were in the temple area and its surrounding fortifications, but reports suggested that it was more than 10,000![18]

I tried to work out just how much food would be eaten every day by 10,000 hungry men, but the numbers were too big, so I just gave up and collected whatever I could. However, I made sure that I was careful, never forgetting that my activities would be very interesting to the Romans. If they found out what I was doing, heavy punishment would be certain.

It is the only time I can ever remember being glad that God had not given us children.[19]

At least I didn't need to worry about getting the food into the temple itself – I could leave that to others, and hope that my Samuel would get the food he needed to help protect God's temple from the Romans.

My task would help him, and I would pursue it with faith and all the strength that Yahweh, our God, provides.

---

[18] Josephus reports that at the end of the siege, 12,000 Jews were killed (Josephus, The Wars of the Jews, Book 1, Chapter 7, section 5).
[19] The Bible does not tell us whether or not Anna had children. None are mentioned.

But how was I to collect such large amounts of food without the Romans noticing? I decided that the collection had to happen in the market areas of the city. Large quantities of food would already be passing through each day, so my planned activities shouldn't draw undue attention. Obviously, I couldn't afford to *buy* all of the food that would be needed, but I planned to visit people all over the city and convince them of just how important the food collection was for God's temple.

For me, the main problem was the factions within the city. I was supporting the defence of the temple, plain and simple, but it was hard to do that without being viewed as supporting Aristobulus, and I knew that my husband had little time for him or his ambitions. On the other hand, Hyrcanus was no better – he was even willing to let a Roman commander take over Jerusalem and the temple! Unfortunately, we can sometimes be seen by others as taking sides in political squabbles, even though the specific goal that we are pursuing may be only incidental to the better-known cause. For Samuel, the goal was godliness and the immediate task was to protect the temple from being profaned by Romans or corrupt Jews. I agreed with him. I still do. In asking people to give food, I tried to emphasise that it was work being done for Yahweh – but most people saw me as being on Aristobulus' side. Some of Hyrcanus' followers were willing to be convinced and helped me as they were able, but most treated me with suspicion or even as an enemy to be worked against.

I am told that it has always been so amongst us Jews as a people: we concentrate on human leaders instead of on the Most High God. We watch constantly for a Messiah, or the coming son of David, but keep on being let down by leaders who seek only their own fame and power. I'm sure that the baby I saw today will be better. Apart from anything else, his parents are very different from the rich, proud, self-seeking parents of most of the leaders who keep trying to take control of God's people. When the Roman legions under Pompey threatened us, Aristobulus and Hyrcanus spent at least as much time fighting each other as they did trying to fight the Romans. But I couldn't let it get me down or stop me from gathering food to help the people who really were doing something to save the temple. I also did my best to encourage generosity with food donations.

All over the city I travelled during those two or three months, visiting many houses and speaking to thousands of people. Lots of other women helped me, and huge amounts of food were collected and delivered to the men in the temple. I don't know how the delivery was achieved, but it seemed to work.

Never did the Romans seem to suspect anything. Never was I questioned about my daily work collecting food all over the city. Never did they ask why I delivered so much food to the market area near the temple, nor who the busy men were to whom I gave it. Somehow, these men managed to consistently deliver it to the brave defenders who still resisted every attempt to take the temple area.

Unfortunately, the Romans showed no signs of giving up either, nor of trying to negotiate an end to the impasse. Maybe they didn't see it as an impasse at all, but rather as a necessary series of steps that they had to take to achieve an inevitable victory.

All that time, Pompey's men were busy filling in the valley to the north of the temple and bringing heavy battering rams and other siege equipment from Sidon.

On several occasions, they tried to bring their rams up to attack the walls around the temple, but the defence from our soldiers was too strong. So then they did what people have been doing for hundreds of years: they used our dedication to our religion against us. The Sabbath is a wonderful observance, but it has caused many problems when the nation is under attack. Many years ago, our soldiers refused to fight on the Sabbath, and so our enemies always attacked on that day, when they knew they would meet with no resistance. Many a brave warrior was slaughtered where he stood, defenceless.

After one particular massacre, our regulations were altered to allow individuals and armies to take defensive action even on a Sabbath – but *only* defensive action. That was how things stood when Pompey was trying to conquer the temple. When he could not move his battering rams into place to attack the walls because of the ferocious defence, he withdrew them, and for a couple of days nothing happened. Now it may have been just a coincidence, but I doubt it. I think it is much more likely that some smart advisor saw an opportunity to take advantage of our religious piety. When the Sabbath came, the Romans began again to manoeuvre their battering rams into place. They made no attempt to attack the walls while doing so, nor did they have soldiers placed to defend the workers as they brought up the rams and other assault equipment. They knew they were safe.

To add insult to injury, as the morning passed with no attacks from the defenders who were quietly watching from the walls, the Romans began to smile and laugh and wave to them!

Now, how should we follow our religion when our enemies take advantage of us like that? Some say that if only we have faith, God will care for us – and I might agree with them if we as a nation were in better standing with God. If we had been righteous, maybe we really could demand God's support, but when our nation has so consistently gone its own way over the centuries, will such a desperate faith help when judgement comes? Most of the nation only wants God's help when they can't achieve what they want by themselves. Our keeping of the Sabbath feels more like following a set of rules than viewing as a delight the opportunity to contemplate God's holiness.[20] As an old woman, I now see very clearly that much of our religion is just empty ritual, and so it was back when Pompey attacked – much the same as when Isaiah described it so long before as "empty offerings".[21] I didn't see it quite as clearly when I was young, but even then I had enough questioning to doubt that God would feel bound to protect our nation in every conflict! I didn't really want to think about it, but I couldn't help wondering whether God might be using the Romans to punish us, as he had used the Babylonians.

On that particular Sabbath, the progress of the Roman preparations was swift but methodical, and nobody did anything to stop it. The Roman soldiers worked hard, while the Jewish defenders concentrated on their worship. Only a few defenders watched, clearly frustrated by their inability to stop the inexorable preparations for an attack. As the sun

---

[20] Isaiah 58:13
[21] Isaiah 1:11-14

swung lower in the sky, the battering rams were ready in position, and the siege towers were there too. The Romans began to take much more care, knowing that, for the defenders, the new day would begin at sunset, at which time their opportunity for unopposed action would be over. The soldiers hurried into position, hoping to be ready for an attack just before the defenders were freed from their self-imposed cease-fire.

In the end, the two sides were ready for action at almost exactly the same time. The sun set, and immediately the defenders tried to disable the battering rams, which were just swinging into action, by dropping heavy stones from the defensive positions onto the battering rams and the soldiers who were urging them on. But many of the stones just bounced off the shields that had been erected over the rams.

As darkness fell, the sounds of battle filled my ears. I prayed that God would help the dedicated soldiers who defended his house. I had hope, but no certainty.

Instead, I had a horrible feeling that the battle would be decided before morning.

☙

I have never known another night like that night. There was no way to know what was happening in the battle for the temple. Darkness shrouded the hilltop, though from time to time eerie, leaping flames lit the scene. With the constraints of the Sabbath removed, the defenders set to work urgently heating pitch, which they lit and poured down on the attackers as rivers of fire, hoping to consume the huge logs that were battering their defences. Apparently one ram was badly damaged in this way, but the others remained unscathed, free to continue their terrible work.

Sleep was impossible, and there was nothing that I could do but pray. I could feel the dull thud as the battering rams repeatedly struck the defensive walls. These walls were strong enough that they had been able to resist an 8-month siege just a few years earlier, but they were not built like the walls of the city herself. They could not resist the determination and modern equipment of Rome.

At times the rhythm altered or stopped entirely, as one or more of the battering rams reached another milepost in dismantling the walls. Arrogant Gentiles were remorselessly battering their way into God's temple. I still remember my fervent prayer that God would do again in my days what he had done to the Assyrian army when it had thought to take over God's temple. But despite the prayer, I was filled with doubt, because the contrast between Hezekiah and our current leaders could not have been more marked. Nor were there any prophets like Isaiah available – it seemed that God had withdrawn from his people. Since God always keeps his promises, I was sure that he could not have abandoned the descendants of Abraham, Isaac and Jacob. If he had withdrawn from us, it must have been because we had first withdrawn from him.

I was afraid that we stood on our own against the Romans – and the events of that horrific night did nothing to change my mind.

The night seemed as long as a week, and my ever-present fear turned to terror on several occasions when the sound of falling masonry was clearly heard and the noise of battle swelled for a time. Yet each time, the noise level dropped again after a while and the familiar rhythm of attack returned. For the time being, abject terror receded, and the gnawing fear that had been with me for three months returned. And still the night dragged on.

It was just before dawn that I felt a particularly heavy thud from a ram, followed by the thunder of falling stones. My heart leapt into my mouth as the sound of shouting swelled, louder and louder. I didn't know what to do, but I could no longer stay where I was, doing nothing, so I ran, unthinking, towards the temple.

Before I arrived at the surrounding Roman wall, though, I had begun to think again, and slowed to a walk. Pink was beginning to tint the clouds to the west and east, and I knew that before long it would be light. The sounds of desperate fighting were easily audible, muffled though they were by the Roman defences. I turned and retraced my path a little way to the house of a wealthy man whose wife had generously provided large quantities of food for the temple. The second storey of their house commanded a clear view of the temple, and I hoped that I would be able to see what was happening. True, it was early, but surely no-one could be sleeping as this horror unfolded in the temple!

It was still dark in the streets as I approached the door and knocked, but a servant girl quickly opened the door. I recognised her.

"Greetings, Abigail," I said. "Is your mistress available?"

"It's very early to come visiting, missus."

"Yes, but this is no ordinary day," I agreed, looking over my shoulder as the noise of battle continued to increase. It had become so loud that I wondered if the fighting had spilled out beyond the Roman containment walls. Lights were flickering in the windows of most houses in the street, and several doors were opening cautiously. "Abigail, please check whether I can see Miriam," I pleaded.

"Alright," began the girl, but then a worried voice came from behind her.

"What's going on, Abigail? Why is the door open? Who is... oh, it's you, Anna."

"Yes, Miriam," I replied, "I'm worried about what's happening in the temple. The noise keeps getting worse. I wanted to find a place from which I can see. Your upper rooms have a good view of the area. May I come in?"

"It's too dark to see much yet," Miriam answered. "I've been watching myself."

"It will soon be fully light."

"True – and I'm afraid of what we'll see once it is. But come in."

I entered the house and the door was closed and barred behind me. We climbed together to the upper room, where windows faced towards the temple. The shutters were already open. Clouds suffused with red and pink formed a serene backdrop that seemed somehow inappropriate as the garish yellow of leaping flames below and the overwhelming noise of conflict filled the senses.

As we looked through the window, we were able to see over the new Roman wall, but the gloom of night still hid most of what was happening beyond. Where flames lit the scene, I could see hand to hand fighting. Clearly the defensive wall that surrounded the temple area must have been breached somewhere nearby.

Daylight stole imperceptibly across the scene, and the fringes of the clouds changed slowly to gold. Day was upon us, and suddenly another thundering crash came from further to the north, followed by the horrifying roar of falling rubble. In the growing light, we could see thousands of Roman soldiers moving towards the section of the temple wall from which the sound seemed to have come.

Had the defence crumbled completely? What was happening to the defenders – to Samuel? I felt completely helpless. Desperate prayer was the only option available, but already my prayers were failing me. The defences that I had asked God to strengthen had fallen as I watched, and the Romans were closing in relentlessly.

I watched for much of the day, and the terrible sights I saw remain seared into my mind. It was a day that challenged my faith in God more than any other before or since.

Roman soldiers captured the temple, easily overcoming all resistance. Their armour protected them from the limited weaponry of the defenders, and their swords and spears made their brutal slaughter of the Jewish defenders seem almost casual and businesslike. This was no response of angry revenge, nor a savage reaction to a fear-filled conflict that has got out of control: rather, it was a clinical and methodical extermination, as when a householder systematically removes unwanted insects from his home.

By noon, the fighting was over and thousands of Jewish fighters lay dead in the temple area they had tried to defend. Even the priests who had been offering the morning sacrifice had been cut down as they worked, making no attempt at all to defend themselves, and many other defenders had committed suicide in preference to being captured and having to see the degradation of that holy place.

Yet that was not the end of the mayhem.

Thousands more of the defenders had been rounded up and now stood, sullen and silent, in the temple courts, under the watchful eyes of their conquerors. It was at this time that the divisions among us Jews were highlighted in an utterly disgusting manner. Most of the defenders were supporters of Aristobulus, and when the Romans had had their fill of slaughter and assembled the survivors together, Hyrcanus' supporters joined the Romans, mocking and sneering at their defeated brothers. The captives apparently responded with outspoken contempt of their own, and abuse flowed back and forth. Tempers on both sides flared, but the captives were restrained and unarmed. Hyrcanus' supporters were not.

It was said later that as many Jews died from the angry knives of their fellow Jews as had died from the impersonal swords of the Romans.

About 12,000 Jews died that day. I never found out how my Samuel died – whether at the hand of cold-blooded Romans or treacherous Jews.

Either way, at 25, I was a widow.

It was three days before I was able to confirm that Samuel was dead, and I never saw his body. A friend of his who survived assured me that Samuel had been well early in the morning – before the Roman battering ram had broken through the wall of the tower. That had been the loudest of the sounds that I had heard as day was breaking. The tower had collapsed and taken some of the fortifications with it. For the Romans, the falling masonry had opened a path into the temple compound. For the defenders, it had opened the floodgates of death.

Samuel had loved God's temple and had been willing to give his life defending it. But had his sacrifice achieved anything?

Aristobulus and Hyrcanus were brothers, as are the Sadducees and Pharisees, yet brotherly hatred had left our nation enslaved.

Thousands of widows like myself reaped the rewards of that hatred, and for several months I fought against the temptation to let hatred take over my heart as well.

Seven years of marriage was all too short. How, I wondered, could God have let my Samuel die? Now I had no husband, and no child to remember him by either. I felt utterly alone.

In the 60 years that have followed, I have tried to concentrate on my relationship with God. At first it was an unbearable struggle, but slowly I learned acceptance and possibly even a little understanding.

God promised that if his nation obeyed his laws, they would always receive blessings, growing ever more powerful as a nation. Exile to Assyria and Babylon had come because of disobedience, but it seemed that the returning exiles had learned little from their punishment.

Divisions between brothers had led to a struggle for power so bitter that both sides were willing to enlist foreign help over many years. For most of the participants in the struggle, the temple, and men like my husband Samuel, were only tools. Could a nation that behaved like this ever expect God's help?

Surely, I felt, if God's help was to be given at all, it would not be to Aristobulus or Hyrcanus, to Sadducees or Pharisees? Surely God's help would come another way – a humble, holy way.

Samuel's death still saddens me, but at least I know that he had a hope for the future – and I think that I have now been blessed to see the first step of that future arriving....

༄

After taking the temple, Pompey entered its inner sanctuary. People who were not even Jews, let alone priests, invaded the holy places of God's sanctuary – but maybe God didn't care. Perhaps my own people had already made God's temple so unholy that a few extra foreigners couldn't make much difference. I don't know. God knows. What I do know is that Pompey didn't profane our temple permanently. Imagine, he could have turned it into a pagan temple! Instead, within just a few days, he had done his best to consecrate the temple again. The Roman soldiers were removed and the temple was handed back to the Jews with astonishing speed. Of course, the people it was handed over to were the very ones who had not considered it worth defending from the Romans in the first place!

There aren't many people now who know much about the political situation back then. Today, the Pharisees are presented as holy and righteous, dedicated to the temple, and they suggest that the Sadducees have always been rich, money-centric and interested in the temple only for the power it gives them. How the years have hidden the truth!

Few believe me when I tell them that it was the Sadducees who defended our temple from the Romans.[22] I smile when I ask them who they think would be willing to die fighting for the temple, because I know that they will answer me confidently but incorrectly, assuring me that only the Pharisees would show such holy courage.

Yet it was Hyrcanus and the Pharisees who welcomed the Romans into Jerusalem.

The Sadducees stood against the might of Rome. It was Sadducee blood that stained the pavement as Roman soldiers and their helpers, the Pharisees, ran amok. Sadducees stood unbowed among the broken walls and gave their lives for the love of Yahweh's temple.

The oh-so-holy Pharisees helped the Romans. The godly Pharisees slaughtered their fellow Jews in anger and hatred – and our people have been in slavery ever since, betrayed by the Pharisees. So much for their much-vaunted holiness: power was more important to them.

Maybe times have changed – I don't know.

In the defence of the temple, there were also some who, like Samuel, fought alongside the Sadducees just because it was the right thing to do. Samuel was no Sadducee or supporter of Aristobulus, but he wasn't a Pharisee either, unwilling as he was to support Hyrcanus. Samuel loved God and his temple – he was always very cautious of human organisations. We shared the same love, and once the temple

---

[22] See https://www.livius.org/articles/concept/roman-jewish-wars/ (para 3) and https://www.newworldencyclopedia.org/entry/Pharisees (Background, para 6)

was given back to the Jews, I couldn't keep away from the place where my husband had worshipped and died.

Over the years that followed, I spent many hours in the temple of God. At first, I was fighting with God and went more to remember Samuel than to worship, but over time, I have found peace and acceptance of the will of God. The temple is a house of prayer, and I ignore the human plots and intrigues that would lead me away from seeking God.

I suppose that we have proved that we, as a nation, will not, *cannot*, serve God properly. So many different forms of leadership, yet not even the godly leaders have been able to keep us close to God for long. Judges have failed, kings have failed, priests have failed and prophets have failed – because, above all, we, the people, have failed.

Yet God has not given up on us – not in more than 1,000 years. How is that for patience?

And now, something new is happening.

There are men and women who have been hoping for years that God will redeem Jerusalem, free us from the Romans and usher in a kingdom of righteousness ruled over by a descendant of David. Prophets like Nathan, Isaiah, Jeremiah and Ezekiel all spoke of this, and now, if you will believe me, it is finally happening.

At times through my life, God has spoken to me, so that some call me "Anna the prophetess", but today he showed me his work without saying a word. A little child, a cute and delightful baby, was brought to the temple today. He looked like just the sort of baby Samuel and I dreamed of having, but could not have, so long ago.

Almost 6 weeks old, he was smiling and happy, and his parents, a thoughtful but joyous couple, were just the same. They had brought him to the temple at the time for purification of his mother and to present him to God as was commanded for all firstborn sons.

Simeon was there with them, brought at that time by the hand of God, even as I was. We have often spoken together about the Messiah and longed for his appearing. Simeon is an old man, righteous and devout – just the sort of man that I hope Samuel would have been if he had lived to old age. Together we marvelled at this child. Simeon had been told that he was Yahweh's anointed, the Messiah we have been waiting for.

It is hard to picture that little baby, all gurgles and chuckles, grown up to be a king! It is also hard to imagine all of the difficulties that his parents will have to go through, trying to be worthy parents of the Messiah. Imagine having a child who, from an early age, can identify your failures and notice when you do not practice what you preach!

Simeon blessed the parents, but specifically warned the baby's mother that the child is to be a sign that is opposed and that a sword would pierce her heart.

When I heard that warning, it struck me that righteous people have always been opposed, and many such have died by the sword through the history of my people – prophets and priests as well as ordinary men and women. Would the Messiah...? I pushed the question aside – it was ridiculous. The Messiah was going to be a victor, a king who could overcome opposition. Only a small voice of questioning refused to be quieted, prompting me to think of Isaiah's words about a suffering servant; but enough of that: it was time to rejoice.

The child was still jigging contentedly in his mother's arms, blissfully unaware of the significance of Simeon's serious words, but his parents were looking grave.

We spent some time together there, mulling over the wonder of the work of God, and how suddenly his words from olden times could come to life in front of us.

"Sir," said the baby's father to Simeon, "you said that now you have seen God's salvation. Were you referring to our baby, Jesus?"

"Yes. In little Jesus I have seen the salvation of God. Salvation not only from our enemies, but also from our sins."

"Defeat and utter destruction is coming for the Romans at last," I said, eagerly.

"I don't think so," mused Simeon. "This salvation has been prepared in the presence of all peoples and is a light to the Gentiles. Yes, there will be glory for Israel, but not utter destruction of the Gentiles." He paused for a moment, his brows furrowed, then shook his head before continuing, "This is not how I pictured the work of the Messiah, yet these words came from God."

"Remember that this temple is to be 'a house of prayer for all nations,'" I said, quoting from the words of Isaiah, "but it has never truly been that yet."

"Will my baby really be a light that reveals Yahweh to the Gentiles?" asked Mary, her eyes wide.

"It seems so," said Simeon, gently.

Mary and Joseph looked at each other, and then at Jesus, wonder in their eyes.

"We knew that he was a special baby," said Joseph. "Mary was told many things by an angel of God before Jesus was even conceived, but to be a light to the whole world means that he is even greater than we thought."

"Maybe he will be able to lead all the world to Yahweh," I suggested, and as I said it, the idea felt right.

"But don't forget about the sword that I mentioned," said Simeon, looking at Mary with compassion. "Your task will not be easy, but still – you are very blessed."

We continued to share our thoughts and hopes about God's plans for this baby, and the young couple told us more about what angels had said to them months before, and also to some shepherds on the night Jesus was born. Mary then spoke of the son born miraculously to an aged priest and his barren wife – a birth that had been announced beforehand by an angel in this very temple.

"Was the priest's name Zechariah?" asked Simeon.

"Yes," said Joseph. "He is of the priestly division of Abijah. His wife Elizabeth is Mary's cousin."

"And wasn't he unable to talk after the angel spoke to him?" I asked. "We heard that he came out of the holy place looking terrified – couldn't say a word!"

"Yes, that's true," answered Mary, eagerly; "at least, he couldn't speak until after the baby was born and he had named him 'John' as the angel had commanded. Thankfully, after that he was able to speak again."

I left the temple wondering at the events happening around me. God's angels had been very active over the last year or so, visibly working with people in unusual ways. That too must show just how important this baby was. If only he had come when I was a baby: Samuel and I would have been glad to serve God's chosen Messiah; pleased to help him replace Aristobulus and Hyrcanus and all of the other self-serving leaders we have endured. But at least I have been able to see him.

Thank you, God, for sending your anointed one to save your people. Thank you for letting me see him – the fulfilment of all of your glorious future plans for the world, wrapped up in an innocuous bundle of cloths. So delightfully cute, but still far too young to understand just how important he is to become.

He will learn. He will learn.

Thirteen

Preparing the Way

For the true story see Matthew 3, Mark 1:1-11; Luke 3:1-22; John 1:19-34.

I was born into a poor man's family in Galilee.

It was a religious home, but not in the ways of the Pharisees – we weren't rich enough for that. My parents had a simple, practical faith in God. They tried to obey his laws, attended the synagogue regularly and went to the temple in Jerusalem three times a year. As a family, we spoke often of the beauty of God's creation and the certainty of his love for Israel. We prayed for the Messiah. We looked forward to the feasts in Jerusalem and enjoyed them when they came.

My father worked hard. So did my mother. They taught me to work hard, too, and to appreciate God's blessings and care.

As I left childhood behind, I learned my father's trade and began to make my own choices.

This led me to John the Baptist.

One year when I was in Jerusalem for the Feast of Booths, many people were talking about a priest called John who didn't work in the temple but stayed out in the desert or baptised people in the Jordan. It took me a while to work out what this "baptising" was, but once I did, I wanted to go and hear what the man said, and maybe watch him baptising.

I was very glad that I had gone. John spoke a message that had a ring of truth. An urgent message that people should be baptised with a "baptism of repentance" – so much so that people were starting to call him "John the Baptist". Standing in the Jordan River and talking to the crowds, he would baptise any who were willing to confess their sins and repent.

Of course, his message only appealed to people who weren't already convinced that they were righteous. People who believed that they had no need of repentance naturally felt no need for John either.

Yet for many of the common people who knew within themselves that there was something wrong in their life that separated them from God, John's message struck a chord. For any who wanted to change their life and walk with God, John offered a solution.

The Pharisees tend to put people in two categories: those, like themselves, who had been righteous from birth; and sinners, born in sin and living lives steeped in sin, who could never really bridge the gap that lies between themselves and God.

John told us about repentance and a change that could lead to salvation. He also made it clear that such a change was needed by everyone, including the Pharisees. As you can imagine, they weren't happy with that!

I had always tried to obey God's commands, but I could never satisfy the picky, technical requirements of Pharisees that seemed to require that people be born into the right families – rich, powerful families – to be righteous. Nor could I ever satisfy myself that I was righteous – I was too well aware of my failings and how I sinned in both what I did and what I thought. The law and the prophets taught me that clearly, and convinced me that I could never satisfy the law's requirements on my own. *Wanting* to do better was easy. Actually *being* better was where it all went wrong. But John gave us all some practical examples of how we could live godliness. It made sense. It sounded like the sort of life that would avoid the criticisms God had made of Israel through his prophets over hundreds of years. Prophets like Isaiah and Jeremiah, and even Malachi who spoke after the return from exile, had all criticised our nation for pursuing a religion that concentrated on "religious activities" rather than on how people actually lived.

It made sense, and I felt that I had failed just as the nation had failed. I knew that I needed to concentrate on that aspect of my worship, so I repented and was baptised by John. As I came up out of the water, there was a wonderful feeling of release from sin. But with it came the certainty that I also needed to show that I had been changed and wanted a different life.

That very day, I met a man who had heard of John's teachings and had come in the hope of receiving help. He was poorer than I, and had no cloak. So I put what I had learned into practice, and gave him my cloak – after all, I had another at home and would not die of cold before I got there. It was a simple action, but I knew that it would help a man who needed help, and please God. And pleasing God was more important to me then than it ever had been before.

I stayed for several days longer, listening to the powerful, practical teachings of John. Then as I was sitting beside the river one day, a man came to be baptised and John tried to put him off, saying that he shouldn't baptise him.

Naturally, that got my attention. I had heard John condemn the Pharisees as a brood of vipers who needed to produce fruit that showed their repentance, but his response to this man was quite different from that.

Amazingly, John said that this man should be baptising him, not the other way around. So what was different about him? I was intrigued, but couldn't hear what was being said properly, so I quickly slid off the bank into the water and hurried closer.

Neither of them was trying to make a grand presentation of their discussion, so I had to get quite close to listen.

I'm afraid that that almost sounds as if I was eavesdropping on their conversation, but it wasn't like that either. It was no whispered, secret conversation, but a discussion that you might have where you don't mind if anyone hears it, but that only your closest friends would really care enough to want to come and listen to.

I wasn't a close friend of either of them, but I had already decided that, if possible, I did want to become John's friend.

Anyway, I waded across to them just in time to hear the man say quietly to John that it was proper for them to do what he requested to "fulfil all righteousness".

I didn't understand what that meant, but when the man again insisted that John should baptise him, John obeyed.

Now John wasn't proud – how could he be when he wore clothes made of camel's hair? – but he did his work with confidence. He knew exactly what God wanted him to do and was not going to be distracted from it. I certainly hadn't seen him listen to anybody else before when they tried to tell him how he should be doing his job. You may find it strange, but I had seen quite a few leaders try to tell him what he should be doing in the few days I had been watching him. They had come to see what could be done about this popular preacher. Maybe I am too cynical, but it seems to me that while many popular leaders start with good intentions, good hopes and good plans, they are *always* subverted into less honourable directions by one of two things: pride or money. The existing leaders had come to see if they could subvert John and redirect his popularity to their own ends.

But John wasn't having any of that, and that impressed me. Although I had only been around him for a few days, it was one of the things that made his teaching so much more convincing. He said that he was not important: not the Messiah; not the son of David; not the coming king; not the prophet Moses had spoken of – instead, he was just a servant, preparing the way for the Lord.

So now I was fascinated to see what was happening with this man. For some reason, it seemed as if it might be important.

John baptised the man while I stood nearby and watched. It was just the same as when he baptised me and the hundreds of other people I had watched him baptise, except that John seemed to be treating him with great respect. I wondered why. Whatever the reason, though, I had enough respect for John that if he considered a man worthy of respect, I was willing to start with a good opinion of the man myself.

The man came up out of the water and didn't even stop

for a discussion with John. Instead, he waded to the bank and walked away a short distance. I observed that John was still watching him, so I watched him myself. The man stopped and stood still, looking up to the sky as if he was praying.

Then some strange things happened. A bird fluttered down and landed on the man and stayed there. That was strange enough, but then, a loud, deep rumbling voice came from the sky. You could almost have thought it was thunder, but I heard the words distinctly as if they were an answer to the man's prayer: "You are my beloved son; with you I am well pleased."

The echoes of that deep voice faded, and the man walked away.

It was all over so quickly that I could almost have thought that I imagined it. I looked across questioningly at John and found that he was still watching the man as he walked away. Seeming to feel my gaze, John turned around and met my eyes: "I saw the Spirit descend from heaven like a dove, and it remained on him," he said to me pensively. "I myself did not know him, but he who sent me to baptize with water said to me, 'He on whom you see the Spirit descend and remain, this is he who baptizes with the Holy Spirit.' And I have seen and have borne witness that this is the Son of God."

I looked back to see where the man was, but he was gone, swallowed up in the crowd.

The Son of God?

I still wasn't sure what it meant, but I was convinced that I had to stay with John and learn more about his message and what this man had to do with it all. My work could wait; this was much more important. Much more urgent, too.

Fourteen

A Samaritan Wedding

For the true story, see John 4:5-43. This story goes far beyond the details in the gospel and describes a possible result of the woman's discussions with Jesus.

I'm getting married today.

Generally if someone told you that, it would conjure up in your mind a picture of a young couple joining their lives together and sailing off into the happy waters of married life, learning its ups and downs together.

But it's not like that for us.

Neither of us is new to marriage.

My wife to be, Shufrina, has been married five times before: widowed once, and divorced four times.

My marital history is similar.

When we met, we were both unattached – at least in our own minds. I'll say more about that later.

Shufrina was 34 years old at the time, and I, 35. We were both jaded with the idea of marriage. It just hadn't worked out for us. We found each other attractive, but we weren't going to get tied up with another marriage. After all, we were both used to the idea that relationships don't last. So we decided to live together without the formality of marriage.

In Judea, that could easily have got us stoned, and even here in Samaria it caused many raised eyebrows and meant that many people no longer talk to us.

We didn't care – or not much, anyway. We merely dismissed our critics as old-fashioned fuddy-duddies or religious cranks. We were happy to live our way and let them live theirs. Why wouldn't they do the same?

Life continued, and our relationship would probably have lasted another year or two if it hadn't been for Jesus.

Yes, it was Jesus who changed things for us.

I'd never heard of him until Shufrina came home from the well one day and said that she had met a man who told her everything she had ever done. Well, that didn't sound good to me, but she was very impressed by it.

Shufrina told me that she had found a Jew sitting quietly beside the well. He didn't look dangerous, so she went to draw water. Then, just as she began to lower the bucket into the well, he asked her for some water.

"What, a Jew asked you for water?" I interrupted, amazed.

"Yes, he really did, and when I questioned it he said that if I had known who he was, I could have asked *him* for water. In fact, a bit later he told me to go and get you too," she said, laughing her gurgling laugh.

I shook my head and replied, "You're talking in riddles, Shufrina. Explain yourself."

"Well, he basically told me that our religion is a confused mess, whereas the Jews actually know what they are worshipping."

"He could be right about the first part," I said. I've never had much time for our religion – it seemed to be more a patchwork of bits of other people's religions than anything genuine. But I also knew that I was no judge of what would be good or bad in a religion! At the same time, I knew that Shufrina was actually quite religious in her own way.

"At first I thought it was just Jewish arrogance, so I guess I started looking for an argument. I think he could tell, and that was why he told me about myself – just to shock me and slow me down. You know, trying to get me to listen."

"What do you mean, 'told you about yourself'?"

"He told me to go and get my husband."

"Ouch! A Jew asking that? Did you admit the truth about us?"

"Sort of. At first I said that I had no husband."

"I suppose you don't, legally, although surely our relationship is something like marriage?"

"You know that neither of us wanted the restrictions of marriage, just the...."

"Yes, yes, yes," I interrupted again. "Well what did he say then?"

"He said that I was telling the truth, and that I had had five husbands and that the man I had now was not my husband."

"How did he know that? Had you been talking to anyone before he came? Had he heard you?"

"No, it wasn't like that. There was no-one there when I arrived except him. He was just some random Jew as far as I was concerned. I can tell you that it was a bit embarrassing to have it stated out loud that the man I was living with was not my husband. I was glad there wasn't anybody else there."

"Sounds like a typical judgemental Jew to me! What has it got to do with him?"

"I felt the same way, and that's why I decided to ask him one of the questions that are always causing fights between Samaritans and Jews: where should we worship? He told me that there was a time coming when we wouldn't worship God either here or in Jerusalem, and he went on to say that God was looking for true worshippers. But he didn't call him 'God' most of the time, he called him 'the Father', which intrigued me."

"You're way too worried about religion," I answered. "Can't you see that it's just a way for people to try and control you?"

"I'm sure that you're right about a lot of religion, but somewhere there has to be a God who created us; humans can't make that up!"

"I suppose not. So what did he tell you?"

"He told me a lot about worshipping the Father in spirit and in truth. He seemed to be suggesting that this worship needs to replace the sort of worship that is based on having a big argument about where we should worship. I think his point might have been that *how* we worship is more important than *where* we worship. He was saying that God – sorry, 'the Father' – wants us to worship him because we understand him, not just for appearance."

I laughed a bit at that. "That won't go down well with either our priests or the Jewish priests," I said. "The way they parade around in their fine clothes with their noses in the air makes it pretty clear what their worship is all about. They like showing off and looking down on people like us."

"Well, this man wasn't like that. After all, he was willing to talk to me."

"And why shouldn't he be?" I asked aggressively. "It's not as if you're a prostitute or a murderer!"

"No, and he didn't comment any further about us not being married, but the fact that he knew it made me feel guilty. After all, I know the Ten Commandments and other things. Remember: 'You shall not commit...' "

Yet again, I interrupted. You see, I wasn't completely comfortable with our situation either, despite the fact that we had both gone through – many times – all of the logical reasons why it wouldn't make sense to get married when we had each had so many failed relationships. "What else did he say?" I asked.

"Well, after he'd talked briefly about the time coming when we would all worship in spirit and in truth, I wanted to show that I knew something – and I suppose I wanted to keep him quiet too – so I said that when the Messiah came, he would explain everything to us. And then he said that *he was the Messiah*."

"But that's ridiculous," I said, in some relief. "Everyone knows that the Messiah will be a king, not a strange Jew who talks to silly Samaritan women."

"Silly?" Fire flashed in Shufrina's eyes, and I grabbed her wrists quickly before she could try to slap me. Her third husband had divorced her because she slapped him once too often. I always made sure that I didn't give her a chance.

"Yes, 'silly'," I said, laughing. "What else could you call someone who says she wants to be religious and then tries to slap her husband all the time?"

"But you're not my husband."

"Ah, we're back to that again."

"Yes. We should get married."

I was surprised. "Why?" I asked.

"Because living together when we aren't married is wrong. It's sin."

"Whoa. Since when have you talked about sin?"

"The fact that I don't talk about it doesn't mean that I don't think about it. After all, you don't talk about it either, but you know that us living together like this is wrong."

"Do I?"

"Yes. You do." She put her hands on her hips and looked at me challengingly. "Don't you?"

I pursed my lips and stood for a moment, staring at her. "I have been a bit concerned at times," I admitted at last. "You see, I met my first wife last week. She's married again, of course, but now she's having problems with her new husband, so she was sounding me out about things. Life as we live it is just a mess. It can't be right."

I let go of her wrists.

"Do you want to go back to her?" Shufrina didn't look happy.

"No. That would be wrong too. A woman can't go back to her previous husband after marrying another man. That's one of Moses' laws that I *do* know."

"So what should you do? What should I do? What should we do?"

"I don't know, Shufrina," I replied, shaking my head. "I need to think. Maybe I need to stop avoiding religion and start looking for answers through it. And maybe this Jew of yours is where I should start looking."

Shufrina gave me a big smile and held out her hand. "Come," she said, and led me out of the door.

We spent the rest of that day listening to Jesus. He's an amazing man. He's not afraid to say what is right and what is wrong, but he also doesn't condemn people who are willing to change, however thoroughly they may have messed up their lives before they met him. Instead, he offers hope – as long as we follow through with the necessary change. His message to anyone who would listen that day was that the kingdom of God is near and so we need to *repent now*. He was very urgent about it, and very convincing too.

There were so many people wanting to listen to him that it was hard to justify trying to get any private time with him, but Shufrina and I were eager to ask him about marriage and so on, since he had brought up the subject with her in the first place. He still didn't condemn us, but he did tell us that divorce wasn't intended in the beginning, at creation,[23] and that it was permitted now only because of our stubbornness. I had to admit to myself that my previous relationships probably would not have broken down if I had been humble

---

[23] Matthew 19:3-9

instead of stubborn. He reminded us of God's laws about marriage and faithfulness, and we were both utterly convinced that we needed to do something to repent; change. But what? When you have messed up one marriage after another, is any real solution possible?

We only had a short time with Jesus, and didn't really get any clear direction as to what we *should* do, apart from that guiding principle: "repent". When we left him we went home together, still unsure what to do in the long term. One thing I was sure of, though, was that we couldn't keep living together when we weren't married, so as we reached home, I opened the door for her and explained that I would go to my father's house and see whether he had anywhere for me to stay.

Over the next few days we discussed the matter and wrestled with our consciences, unable to find any easy solution to our problems. We had lived as though married; should we just separate? We were both terribly sorry for what we had done.

Our previous broken marriages we could not fix, as our partners were married to others now anyway.

What was the best way forward?

Finally we decided that the best solution was to marry and continue our relationship as best we could.

Would Jesus be happy with our conclusions?

We don't know. All we can do is change our ways and hope for forgiveness from God.

So now today is our wedding day, and we plan to live quite a different married life from anything either of us has known before. I do love Shufrina, and we're both working hard on keeping our stubbornness under control.

Life would have been so much easier if we hadn't made all of these bad choices in the first place.

Fifteen

Drink my blood

I have been a follower of Jesus for more than two years now, ever since he was baptised by John the Baptist. I had been baptised by John previously and had decided that I wanted to be his disciple, but then Jesus arrived. I saw John baptise him and watched as the Holy Spirit landed on him in a form that looked like a dove. John told me that this man was the "lamb of God", and even the son of God. That made me want to follow him, but by then he had disappeared.

Nobody seemed to know where he was or even *who* he was, which meant that I couldn't find him.

So for six more weeks I stayed with John, listening to his teaching and admiring his godliness. As a priest, he had a very good background in the law of Moses, yet his application of it was quite different from those of the so-called experts in the law. It seemed to me that if everyone followed his instructions for life, there wouldn't be *any* of the poverty that I saw around. Yes, the nation is full of poor people – I'm one myself – but there is an important difference between being poor and living in poverty.

I have some spare clothes – or at least, I used to have. But real poverty – the grinding, wasting, demoralising, hunger-filled and diseased poverty that dresses men in threadbare clothes, takes away their hope and drives them almost inevitably to theft – this is not common in Judea. John told us how to fix it, and the common people heard him and acted. All it took was a willingness to trust that God would continue to look after us, and then to share anything we didn't immediately need. Of course, one rich person could have given more help than a hundred poor people and never even noticed the cost, but mostly it was only the poor who were willing to listen to John.

That sounds like I'm complaining or blaming the rich, but I'm not. We, the poor, benefitted from taking such action. We chose to trust God for ourselves, and thus became free to help our fellow man. The help was genuinely needed, and it was amazing how much the whole process of helping built or strengthened bonds of friendship. Those who were suffering stopped being "them" and become part of "us".

So the rich kept their money, their worries and their problems. They had to look after it all themselves because they couldn't – or wouldn't – hand either their money or their worries over to God. Paradoxically, the poor won and the rich lost – not that they always saw it that way.

Then the man returned. Apparently he had been out in the wilderness by himself for 40 days. That made me wonder a bit when I thought of the stories I had heard about John being out in the wilderness too. They are both amazing men who care astonishingly greatly for people, yet both have needed to go away from people at times to get closer to God. It's a lesson in priorities that I am still trying to learn.

Anyway, after he returned, I wanted to get to know him. John was again announcing to anyone who showed an interest, that this man was the lamb of God. I followed him and found out that his name was Jesus.

As I said, John was an amazing man, but it didn't take long to find out that this Jesus was even more amazing. John constantly downplayed his own importance and told us to get ready for the one who would follow him. When Jesus came for baptism, John said that this was the man he had been talking about and encouraged us to follow him.

When I met Jesus and got to know him, what stood out to me was his humility. It was just the same as John: he didn't minimise the importance of his work, just of himself as the initiator of the work.

It took me a while to notice it, because I don't tend to pay much attention to what names mean, but the name "Jesus" means "God saves", and it fitted: from the time I met him, Jesus was always trying to emphasise that everything he did was at God's instruction.

Getting to know Jesus was both easy and hard. When I first had the opportunity to talk to him, I noticed that he listened carefully to every word that I spoke. Now I'm not the sort of person that everyone listens to – no great speaker or popular leader – yet Jesus made me feel that I was important to him.

I just greeted him and asked him where he was staying. Based on John's recommendation, I wanted to go and listen to Jesus. He must have something useful to say.

He answered my question and allowed me to follow him and listen to what he said. I quickly learned that he paid the same attention to everyone who spoke to him. He was good at listening to people.

But it took a very short time to learn that he was also good at speaking. I have never heard anyone who could speak as well as he does. I can never hear enough of what he says, yet he does not simply tell me what I think I want to hear. Instead, almost as soon as he says something, I realise that I do want – and need – to hear what he has said.

And I am not the only one who feels like that. First a few, then scores, then hundreds followed him and listened to everything he said.

However, following Jesus was not easy. First there was the punishing physical schedule – up early, then all day spent with growing numbers of people who were looking for help and advice, as well as arguing with determined nay-sayers from time to time, and then late nights spent in prayer or difficult discussions. Second, there was the spiritually demanding nature of interaction with him. He knew what was *in* you, and that was very draining until you learned to relax and make the most of it – but most of his followers never did learn this. Third, there were the challenging things he said, and I'll explain what I mean in a moment.

After a while he chose twelve of us and treated us as his special friends, explaining his teachings to us in more detail and sending us out to spread his teachings to others. It was a wonderful opportunity and taught me even more about relying on God to provide everything that we need. We went out without money or extra clothes or anything like that, and it worked. Any time we needed something, we had it. Everything. Without fail. We also had the right answers to give – God provided those too.

Jesus' audiences kept growing, and they followed him to out-of-the-way places to hear him and kept listening for hours. It became harder and harder for him to move anywhere, so he started going to places that were further and further away from people's homes. If people wanted to listen to Jesus, they had to make a real commitment. At one stage, Jesus went out to a desolate place and, would you believe it, five thousand men followed him out there to listen to him, plus women and children!

At the end of that day, Jesus felt sorry for them and did his most popular miracle of all. Jesus asked us what food we had available. All we could find were five loaves and two fish, yet with those minute morsels, Jesus fed the whole crowd, and there was enough left over to fill twelve baskets with scraps. Jesus was very particular that he didn't want any of the food wasted. Then he sent the crowds away and that was that – or should have been. But it wasn't. The next day, the crowds were busily asking about the miracle and looking for a repeat performance.

That day, Jesus said some of the hardest things he's ever said. Looking back, it's clear that he was trying to separate the real followers from the ones who merely worshipped their stomachs. He talked about eating his flesh and calling it bread. Then he spoke of drinking his blood, something that is utterly beyond the pale. Even we, the twelve who were closest to him, found this very confronting.

Ever since the days of Noah, God has forbidden the eating or drinking of blood. Yet here, the son of God was telling us we had to drink his blood. Many people who had followed him for months could not accept what he said and left.

We couldn't understand it either, but we couldn't leave him. If we left Jesus, where else could we go? There was no other teacher or teaching that was worthwhile, so it was best to stay around, hang on and try to understand what he meant. That day was one of the most difficult days I've ever known, and it was only our trust in Jesus that kept us all with him. We had confidence that he had the words of God; that he was the word of God made flesh.

And now? I still don't understand what he meant, but I'm still willing to trust him. He often speaks in parables and says things that I can't understand until he explains them to us – and even then, I don't always understand. Recently he's started talking about his death, and I don't understand that either.

Following Jesus isn't easy, physically or mentally. He certainly doesn't ever take it easy, and he often doesn't make it easy for us to understand, but if we trust him he does help us. I understand *so* much more about God now than I ever did before, and I could never leave Jesus, whatever happens.

So I'm glad we didn't leave him, but I still don't understand what he says about his death. And as for drinking his blood...

Sixteen

A thankful Samaritan

For the true story, see Luke 17:11-19.

Today, I might be cured.

I wrote those words as soon as I woke up today, and I left them alone on the page. Five words – reflecting both my hopes and my doubts. Then I took them with me as I went out with the others. On waking, I had felt joy and excitement welling up inside me – although I wasn't sure why – and it seemed to grow as I talked to my friends.

Of course, they wouldn't have been my friends if we hadn't all been lepers. They only tolerated me because they were outcasts themselves. We lived together to provide support for each other, and a bit of companionship. They lived at the border of Samaria because they were outcasts from the Jews in Galilee, and I lived at the border of Galilee because I was an outcast from the Samaritans.

Overall, we got on alright, although they clearly looked down on me at times because I was a Samaritan. I tolerated their attitudes because I was interested in God, and their worship of him seemed better than the mixed-up worship I was used to among my own people. True, we claimed to worship the same God, but we mixed him up with so many other gods and so many other ancient traditions from the distant lands of our ancestors that we didn't seem to really understand *what* we worshipped. I knew that I wanted to understand more, and when I caught leprosy, it – perversely – gave me the opportunity to learn more about God. I had to leave my home, my work, my town, my relatives, even my wife and our only son, Joshua. Since then, I've only seen them from time to time, and only from a distance. After all, I don't want either of them to catch this dreadful disease.

So that sheet accompanied me, with its bold, hopeful writing. Those words reminded me not to give up even when we sought Jesus and learned that he must have taken a different road from the one we had expected.

At that point, some of the others suggested that we should just forget about it; give up on our plan. But those words echoed in my mind and reminded me how important our goal had been when I woke up. They made me think just how much it would change my life if it *did* come true. I pictured being with my wife and our son once more; of waking up in the morning and being able to walk among the rest of the people in our village with no need to hide my shame away.

It strengthened my resolve, and I added my voice to the few who said that we should hurry across to the next town to make sure that we got there before Jesus did. And it worked.

There were eight of us who had the energy and courage to go. There were others who had hoped to join us too, but in the end they stayed behind because the effort required was too great. Leprosy is a sickness that is both humiliating and painful. Raw skin is very sensitive – touch it or knock it and it hurts a lot. And suffering saps the will. It is so easy to just stop caring about things, in a way that leaves life merely flowing over one, instead of one *living* life. I've seen it happen with many people over the last two years: newly sick people who never recover from their initial devastation at the diagnosis of leprosy. They stay all day in their shelters and gradually grow more and more morose; hopeless. They give up.

Others never give up, however bad things seem to be. Rufus is such a man, one of those who went with me to see Jesus. He had lost everything because of his leprosy – to the point where he never wants to talk about the way life used to be – but he has never given up hoping for recovery. His was the strongest and most convincing of the voices that spoke in favour of finding Jesus. He caught leprosy as a teenager, and has lost all connection with his family in the 30 years that have passed since. The girl he had been to marry married someone else. His parents were ashamed of his situation and disowned him. His younger brother had been made the heir and ran the family business. Several years ago, when Rufus was badly injured by a rampaging bull and unable to do anything for three months, his family never offered the slightest help, or even acknowledged his plight. If it had not been for the other lepers, he would have been left alone to die of his injuries. Yet Rufus has never given in to depression and never criticises his family for what they did to him.

When you join the "family" of lepers, you are just one more tragic story in a massive collection of tragic stories. Stories of wasted lives and of people who have been abandoned or rejected by their families.

I didn't want it to end that way for me or my friends.

So we set off.

Jesus was travelling along a road that would take him through a town only a few kilometres away from where we lived, and we hurried there. When we arrived, we enquired whether Jesus had arrived yet and were assured that he hadn't. Naturally, we had to stay outside the town, and the townsfolk didn't even want us on the road that led into the town, so we stood off to one side and watched.

As we waited, we met another two lepers who lived outside the town and we all talked about Jesus. They were Jews too, and they weren't very happy with the fact that he had travelled through Samaria at times. They criticised both Jesus and the Samaritans for a while until one of my friends told them that I was a Samaritan too. I'm used to their attitude about us and ignored it, but I was very pleased at the confirmation that Jesus isn't above talking to Samaritans.

Jesus is a Jew, but apparently he's spoken to a few Samaritans and other foreigners, and even healed some. I hoped and believed that he could cure me.

We kept waiting all morning. Some of my friends were ready to give up and go home, but we'd heard that Jesus was often surrounded by crowds that slowed him down, so the rest of us encouraged them to keep waiting. Eventually we heard a commotion along the road, and there he was. A crowd was accompanying him, and it was hard to work out which of the men in the crowd was the one we wanted – his clothes were ordinary, his actions were ordinary, his face was ordinary. Everything about him was ordinary, except for the things he said and the things he could do that no-one else could do.

Obviously, as lepers, we couldn't go close to him, so we stood and shouted from a distance, all ten of us, "Jesus, Master, have mercy on us."

It took quite a while to make ourselves heard; we had to keep on shouting and shouting. If I hadn't been so desperate – and determined – *I* might have given up then.

When at last he heard us and understood what we wanted, all he did was to shout back to us, "Go and show yourselves to the priests."

That's all.

No waving of hands, no bright lights in the sky, just a few shouted words and that was it.

We looked at each other. Nothing had changed. His voice had faded away and there was nothing to show for it. I looked at my skin and it was just the same: raw skin, painful patches.

Jesus hadn't cured us.

But though he said no more, he did keep looking at us. Was he waiting for us to start on our way to Jerusalem? Was there any point in doing so? I thought to myself, "I'm going to look really stupid if I go to the temple and show myself to the priests like *this*!"

Yet when I looked into his eyes, I saw a challenge there. A compassionate challenge.

Start the journey, his eyes were saying, *trust me. Take that first step towards Jerusalem.* He was willing me to do it, but leaving the final decision up to me.

I made my choice. I turned away from Jesus, at just the same time as some of the others did. Together we started to move away, and within a few moments, all ten of us had set off down the road, heading for Jerusalem.

I know it sounds ridiculous, because I had no money, no food, no spare clothes – nothing but faith that it would work. Somehow.

For an hour or more, we walked in silence. No-one had the confidence to ask out loud the questions we all wanted answers to. Some smiled, but most of us were quite unsure of what would happen. By the time we had walked a few kilometres without speaking, my questions were growing more insistent, and I was having difficulty keeping my fears inside me. What if it didn't work? I pressed my lips tightly together and kept walking. Step by step, hill by hill, village by village. It happened so gradually I hardly noticed at first, but as I walked, my skin started to feel... well, different. I looked down at my arms and felt fairly sure that the red patches of raw skin were shrinking. I looked around at my friends and saw them holding up their arms too. Looking. Wondering.

I stopped, and all the others did too. We stood still and each looked at his own skin. Then we looked at each other, and on each face I saw wonder and the beginnings of some of the biggest smiles you could ever imagine.

"It's working," I whispered, and I think my voice was shaking.

Everyone agreed and we all cheered and shouted together. As we stood and jumped and danced in joy and amazement, the healing work of Jesus continued, and after a few minutes my skin was almost like that of a young child, even better than it had been before the curse of leprosy struck me. Immediately, I started to think of my wife; my son; my family; my home.

"Let's go home," said one of my friends.

"We can't do that," another objected. "Jesus said to go to the priests."

"That means Jerusalem, doesn't it? That's a long way."

"There are priests in other towns," said another.

"But they're all down in the south anyway. Not much closer than Jerusalem."

"We're healed. There's nothing for the priests to see. Why bother going to see them?"

"Jesus said to."

"But they wouldn't believe our story anyway. The priests hate Jesus."

"They'll probably find some way to keep saying that we are unclean."

"You're right. We might as well just go home."

Ten people, all given the same instruction and all newly cured of leprosy because they had *started to obey*. Yet now there were as many ideas of what we should do next as there were people in the discussion.

"I think we should go back and say thank you to Jesus," I said.

"But he didn't tell us to do that."

"He wouldn't even talk to you anyway – you're a Samaritan, remember."

"I think he will," I said, "but even if he doesn't, I still want to say thank you and to praise God for what he has done."

"But it'll take you more than an hour to get back there, and then you'll have to find him. It's a waste of time."

"Let's get on with this trip to Jerusalem," said Rufus. He had nothing to attract him to his old home.

"I think I'll just go home," said another.

The discussion went on, backwards and forwards, but I wasn't willing to change my mind. I was going back to find Jesus and thank him.

"I'm going back," I said, finally. Stubbornly.

They gave me their best wishes, but I got the feeling that they were beginning to stand apart from me – even Rufus. Now that we were all healed, they were remembering that I was a Samaritan. It crossed my mind that this might be the last time I saw them. Should I go with them and see if I could maintain the friendship? No! I had to praise God, and tell Jesus how thankful I was. The temple could wait. Even my family could wait one more day. I had to do it.

Well, my friends were right to some extent: it did take quite a while to find Jesus, but it really wasn't bad. He had been travelling along the same road as we were, just more slowly because of the crowds that always demanded his attention.

When I found him, I shouted out my praise to God and explained who I was. Then I fell at Jesus' feet and thanked him. I can never thank him enough for what he has done for me.

Jesus welcomed me, yet he did so in a way that demanded that I acknowledge that I was not a Jew, not one of the chosen descendants of Abraham. He called me a "foreigner", and I suppose I could have got upset about that – but really, it's true. I am a foreigner, not a Jew. Jesus came to teach the Jews, not people like me. However, he still welcomes foreigners like me if we are persistent enough. And he was obviously very happy that I had come back to say thank you and to praise God.

His final words to me were, "Go your way; your faith has made you well."

And if Jesus thought it was a good idea for me to return and say thank you, then I'm sure it *was* a good idea. Now I need to do what he said: go to the temple to offer the gift Moses commanded. I wouldn't have bothered if Jesus hadn't told me to do it, because the Jewish priests are never very happy to see us Samaritans. But since Jesus said it, off I go. What a wonderful day this has turned out to be! Jerusalem first, then home to my family!

I must hurry.

Seventeen

Why won't she help?

For the true story, see Luke 10:38-42; John 11:1-44 and John 12:1-8.

If only I could learn.

It seems such a simple lesson, and Jesus has made it clear that he thinks it's important, but I just can't seem to learn it.

You see, when Jesus visits us, he needs a meal. He always works so hard and must be utterly exhausted at times, the poor lamb. I can't just leave the food to make itself, now, can I?

It's easy to say that listening to him is *more* important, but that's the whole point. What happens to things that are merely important if we spend all of our time on things that are *more* important? Important things are still important, and feeding Jesus is important to me. He speaks truth from God that we all love to hear; he heals people; he refutes the foolish arguments of the Pharisees – and we need all of those things. He deserves to get fed so that he doesn't have to keep on working as a carpenter. He is far more valuable to us as a preacher of righteousness than as a carpenter. At times I have been made very happy by the thought that I am doing the work of God by feeding Jesus.

Yet I also feel that I miss out because my sister Mary won't help me. Instead, she gets all of the benefits that I would so dearly love to have myself.

What a mix-up it all is in my mind!

If Mary would just come and help me for a while, it would only take us away from Jesus for a little time each.

As it is, she gets to listen to Jesus while I'm left straining to hear what he is saying from another room above the sound of bubbling food.

Lazarus, our brother, always goes and listens to Jesus too, and I wouldn't want him helping anyway. He has always been a bit sickly, and after all, it was only two weeks ago that Jesus raised him from the dead after that horrible time when we felt that Jesus had deserted us. Jesus taught me a lesson then too – not to worry about practical details when God is at work. It was Practical Martha lacking faith all over again.

Anyway, it's up to Mary and me to make the food, and that has caused some arguments between us.

I want to give Jesus the best feast that I can arrange, and that means a lot of work. Mary says that she is willing to help with making simple food, but that Jesus would actually prefer a simple meal that allows us to listen to his father's words rather than a feast that has kept us busy with hours of preparation.

Being the oldest, I still feel that the others should obey me, but maybe they have lessons to teach me.

I suppose I should tell you a bit about us. We are three siblings: one brother, Lazarus, and two sisters, Mary and me,

Martha. I am the oldest and the house we live in is mine. I am the practical one – and the one who had to look after the family from an early age when our mother died. Naturally, I was the one who did the cooking, the cleaning, the shopping, the mothering, and everything else around the house while father was out earning the money to buy our bread. Two years later, our father died too, and then life got really difficult. I was still too young to earn any money, and too busy anyway, because the other two are quite a few years younger than me. After a while, we had to sell the house and find a smaller one to live in. I had to be both mother and father, and there was no time for rest or relaxation. No, I worked hard all the time. Slowly, over time, I earned enough money to buy a house of my own – a house in which we three could live together in happiness.

I never had time to find a husband, nor parents or relatives to help me in the search. It's too late now. I run our family instead.

We have always been very close to each other, we three, and close to God as well.

My parents lived in Bethany partly because it was close to Jerusalem. They loved God and enjoyed being near the temple. When they died, we stayed in Bethany because we knew everyone there and were used to being able to visit the temple whenever we wanted to.

Hard work and godliness. Those are the principles that have filled my life – particularly the hard work. It's become a habit, and I always thought it was a good habit until Jesus came along.

It was in the temple that we first met Jesus. He was attending a feast, as all Jewish men must do three times each year.

Jesus is different from other people. The logic he uses isn't practical logic, it's idealistic and completely God-centred – and for people like me, that's difficult. In fact, so far I have found it impossible, but maybe sometime I can start to do better.

I love to listen to Jesus' teaching. I listen all I can, but when food needs preparing, it just can't wait. If I were not the owner of the house, and the leader in the family, maybe I could just let go of the work and leave it undone, but really, who could do that? Jesus is welcomed into the houses of many rich people – I can't feed him and his followers with dry bread and water!

And yes, Mary has already reminded me of the two occasions when Jesus fed huge crowds of people and chose to feed them with bread and fish. No sauces, no condiments, no extra courses, no spices – just bread and fish. I know it's true, but that was outside and in the country. In our own home we have no excuse for feeding Jesus anything less than the very best.

I keep arguing with myself, fighting the obvious. I've been doing so ever since Jesus chided me. Jesus never likes anyone complaining about somebody else's behaviour, so I shouldn't have been surprised at his response. I suspect that I am just trying to dodge the obvious answers that Jesus wants me to come to. I love to listen to his words, but what I keep coming back to is the fact that I think the work really does need to be done.

Now, Jesus told me that Mary had chosen a better option than the one I had chosen. Since I don't think that he objects to the food that I give him, he must be telling me that Mary's priorities are better than mine. And, really, I already know that. It's the very reason I complained. I wanted her to suffer *with* me while we both missed out on listening to him.

But is that the only option? Can I find a way to avoid either of us missing out at all? Maybe I can find a way to prepare the food before Jesus comes. It's true that most of the time we don't know when he is coming until he walks into Bethany or we meet him in the temple – he has to be so careful nowadays to make sure that his enemies don't know where he is going – but I suppose we can normally predict reasonably accurately. He is always in Jerusalem for the major feasts, and I can at least make sure that I am ready then. Ready with food that has already been prepared. It does mean that the food won't be freshly cooked, but there are some recipes that are genuinely better with some time to allow the flavours to mingle.

There must be a way to do this properly – after all, Jesus knows that we need to eat. He didn't come to kill us all with hunger! But he doesn't want food to take us away from listening to the word of God.

Now that I think about it, I once heard that when Jesus went into the desert after he was baptised, he went without food for 40 days. He says that we don't live by bread only, but by the words of God. Those are the words he speaks, the words Mary always makes sure that she hears, and that I just wish I could hear.

It seems that if I want to feed Jesus, I will have to make sure that I can do so without missing out on what he says.

Finally, I think I have the answer.

Simple food, simply prepared – pre-prepared if possible. That's what I need to give. Jesus isn't around for me to listen to very often, so I need to take every opportunity I can.

Eighteen

The plot that failed

For the true story, see Matthew 21:33 - 23:36, Mark 12:1-40 and Luke 20:9-47.

It has been a busy day and no mistake. That uneducated carpenter from Nazareth has been causing trouble again, spreading pernicious rumours about all of the leaders and righteous people in the temple by hiding behind stories.

Early this morning he started out by telling a story about some tenants trying to steal a vineyard by doing away with the owner's servants one by one, and finally killing his son. A ridiculous story, but clearly aimed at us because he has it in for us. I was so angry that I would have loved to drag him away myself and lock him up, or even stone him on the spot, but the ignorant commoners think that he is a prophet and insist that he be treated with respect. Respect! If only he would treat his betters with respect the situation might not be quite so bad!

So we went away and had a quick pow-wow, discussing how we could turn his smart-aleck comments back on his own head. Someone suggested that we ask him a question where whatever answer he gave would be a bad one. It's not hard to think of them – there are lots of paradoxes where neither of the available answers is truly correct.

Well, we tossed ideas backwards and forwards until finally someone suggested the perfect test: ask him whether we should pay taxes to Caesar. Everyone agreed that if he said "No" then he was in trouble with the Romans, and if he said "Yes" then he was in trouble with the patriotic Jews – and that is most of us. It would turn the crowd against him completely.

It wouldn't be hard to get people who would be willing to be witnesses against him if he said that we *should* pay taxes, but it would be a little harder to get him into the trouble he deserves if he said that we *shouldn't* pay taxes. Most people would like that answer – although they probably wouldn't care to carry it out when it came to the crunch.

But the Herodians would be vehemently opposed to any suggestion that we should not pay tax and would be willing to stir up trouble against anyone who suggested it in public. So, just in case Jesus was foolish enough to suggest in the hearing of a crowd of people in the temple that we should *not* pay taxes, we sent a message to some of the Herodians telling them about the little exhibition we had planned. As expected, they were eager to be there – they thought there was a good chance that he would get caught in the trap.

Personally, I thought it was most likely that he would refuse to answer at all, which should be enough to lower his credibility in the eyes of his fanatical followers and the naive commoners who hang on his every word.

The trap was set and I was convinced that we couldn't lose, whatever answer he gave. It couldn't possibly go wrong.

Everything arranged, we headed out into the temple courts again. The Herodians were just arriving as we got to the place where the carpenter likes to harangue the silly mob.

I had been lucky enough to be chosen to ask the question, so I pushed through the crowd until I was near Jesus. It was hard to get through, because it's mostly the uneducated people who cluster around him – the ones who lack most social graces and don't seem to understand that when a learned man needs to get through a crowd, they should move aside promptly out of respect. Being that type, they didn't move, and I was forced to push my way through. Some of the other Pharisees and our followers were with me, as well as those Herodians we had invited along.

I need to point out that I would never normally be seen in public with Herodians, but this was a very special case. Sometimes you need to be willing to take any help you can get – and defeating this wordy carpenter is proving to be just such a case. So, there I was, and the Herodians were with me... Oh! That looks horrible when I write it down! How could I ever be willing to admit that I was with that rabble of pro-Roman sycophants? I'll say instead that they were *near* me, and leave it at that.

I stood in the crowd, resplendent in my robes, phylacteries and other necessary accoutrements, and waited for silence. Of course, I had failed to take into account the fact that this class of crowd just doesn't understand the finer points of social interaction, and their religious background is practically non-existent. Silence never came.

Once it became clear that they were not going to accord me even the most basic courtesy, I realised that I would have to just launch into my little speech without the affected cough and the expansive wave of my hand that I had planned.

Never mind. I knew that it was going to be my hour of triumph. The Nazarene would be taken down a peg through my oratory – even if it was only asking a simple question.

"Teacher," I said, with a nice balance of ingratiating politeness and the calm superiority that showed everyone that I understood that this was a brilliant question, "we know that you are true and teach the way of God truthfully, and you do not care about anyone's opinion, for you are not swayed by appearances." I was very pleased with that sentence, even if I knew that there wasn't a word of truth in it! But it would lull him into a false sense of conceited confidence so that the master-stroke that followed would be completely unexpected: "Tell us, then, what you think. Is it lawful to pay taxes to Caesar, or not?"

I had raised my voice a little for this finale, and I finished the sentence with a beautifully clear enunciation of the final "t" in that last word. It hung in the air, and by that time there really was silence.

Up to that point, everything had been going according to plan, but from then on, things didn't quite work as we had expected. I don't think it was my delivery. My gentle, honey-sweet tone had got everyone's attention just as we predicted, and I'm sure that it had effectively masked the dangerous trap in the question that followed.

But, though Jesus didn't bat an eyelid, there was no doubt that he had seen the trap very clearly. I don't know how he saw through our plot so easily. Without delay, he was on the attack. He called us all hypocrites and accused us of trying to trap him.

In all honesty, I suppose we really were trying to trap him, but it was only for the good of those poor sheep we Pharisees have to look after. I certainly wouldn't be bothering with this wayward woodworker if it weren't for them!

Anyway, I'm sure it was a fluke, but the answer Jesus gave avoided the trap completely. It also *sounded* as if it was an answer to the question, but it wasn't really. Naturally, the ignorant crowd didn't realise it, and they were all amazed at how clever he was and sang his praises – it was positively sickening. Fawning. Drooling over him and laughing at me.

As far as I was concerned, it was the end of any possible reconciliation with him. I have no idea how he came up with such an answer, but it certainly wasn't fair to avoid my question like that.

I left in disgust.

I heard quite a few laughs behind me as I walked away.

Later that day, we heard that the Sadducees had tried their luck with him too. They must have seen or heard of our difficulties and smugly expected to be able to do better. How absurd – as if telling a foolish, concocted story about seven brothers one after another marrying the same woman would ever be clever enough to trap Jesus!

Of course, they got their well-deserved comeuppance. He gave them a stinging rebuke: "You are wrong, because you know neither the Scriptures nor the power of God." There was some truth in that, since the Sadducees are rather ignorant about the Bible. They won't even read most of it! However, it left me with mixed feelings – I was glad to hear they had failed to trap him when we couldn't, but infuriated that he continued to defeat the best minds in the nation. Of course, it must still be blind luck, but it is rather extraordinary.

When we heard of the Sadducees' failure, we couldn't resist the opportunity to highlight Jesus' ignorance on the very day when the Sadducees had failed to do so. It would deservedly improve our standing in the community.

We decided to get another of our number, a scribe he was, to ask the age-old question, "What is the most important commandment in the Law?" People have been arguing about that one for generations, and all the Rabbis express non-binding opinions and then defer to each other so that the question continues to be unresolved.

Well, once again, Jesus showed that he doesn't have the educational background or the sophistication to stand among true rabbis. He deferred to no-one and stated categorically the two commands that he thought were most important. As if we really care about the opinion of an ignorant builder from Galilee!

I admit, however, that we may have chosen the wrong man to ask the question, that time. Not that I have anything against the man, but he is a little liberal and rather too quick to take an argument on its merits instead of considering the context and circumstances or who is involved in the contention. It sadly weakened our case when he simply agreed with Jesus instead of finding a point on which he could quibble.

Never mind, all was still not completely lost, and I'm sure we could have regrouped and reclaimed the high moral ground with just a little more planning.

But Jesus didn't give us the time. It is most disconcerting when a man ignores the basic rules of debate and insists on trying to win at all costs!

Yes, he asked us a fatuous question about whose son the Messiah was. We gave the only answer that anyone can give – the son of David – and he started to insinuate that we had missed a fairly simple clue that would lead us to a different answer. In thinking about it since, I am convinced that he is moving closer and closer to blasphemy.

For us, that was the end of our involvement with the self-styled rabbi for the day and we beat a retreat, our dignity not quite intact, but not completely demolished either.

Later, we heard what he said after we left – imagine that, a public figure slandering us behind our backs! Shameful. All sorts of nasty, unfounded accusations, and made when we couldn't even defend ourselves. If he had said straight out what he was insinuating, of course the crowd would have been on our side, but the ordinary people in the crowds that he collects are a bit slow to pick up on things, and they clearly didn't understand just how ridiculous his suggestions were.

What a day! Embarrassing and infuriating. Jesus is dangerous, and it seems to me that we need to take some very serious steps – and quickly too.

We must get rid of him, whatever it takes...

Nineteen

Guarding the dying

For the true story, see Matthew 27:2-61, Mark 15:1-47, Luke 23:1-56 and John 18:28-19:37.

I've been a centurion for several years, and stuck in Palestine for most of them. It's not a desirable position.

Everybody knows what Palestine and its people are like. It's amazing how such a small group of people can be so well known across a massive empire like ours, but that's how it is. And the Jews are known everywhere as trouble.

Many nations and peoples have been conquered by Rome; it's happened to so many that there's no shame in it. Most use it to their advantage, accepting the empire's cultural and societal benefits while complaining about the taxes they have to pay.

The Jews refuse the benefits, rebel frequently, refuse to cooperate in anything – and complain about the taxes as well.

There is no way that they can successfully rebel against Rome, so why won't they just admit it and quit trying? Can't they see the benefits of gymnasiums and stadiums, roads and security, technology and development? Any sensible nation can – but not the Jews.

It's as if they take a perverse delight in refusing to cooperate! They love to act as if they're holier than anyone else, but then they get into one of their own internal fights and behave worse than we ever do!

Anyway, don't start me on the Jews. I've been here long enough: I know.

Yet I can't really say "don't start me", because it was getting roped into helping with some of their irrational behaviour that prompted me to write a letter to my mother. It's probably easiest if I just include the copy of the letter that I kept. You can ignore the bits at the start, if you want to.

Hi Mum,

How are you going? I hope that the neighbour's baby isn't keeping you awake so much now, and that you have been able to stop Mrs S from gossiping about you. If she's still causing you trouble, tell her that I'm planning to visit later in the year and am not happy with what I hear about her. You know, holding the position of centurion can often be useful in getting troublemakers dealt with.

I'm well, but very tired after lots of hard work over the Jewish Passover festival. The Jews always cause the most trouble around their religious feasts, so the governor has to have lots of extra troops stationed in Jerusalem at such times to make sure things don't get out of hand.

I was there with my men again this year, and I had a very disturbing experience. As you know, I'm not normally into supernatural things. Practical – that's me. OK, I suppose I _am_ a bit superstitious in my preparations for battle, but I haven't been in a real battle for years.

Guarding the dying

Anyway, we were called up from Caesarea to Jerusalem a week before the feast to make sure the troublemakers knew that we were there and in control. Just the normal show of strength that we have to put in place each year.

During that week, there were various disturbances, starting with a man coming into the city riding on a donkey or some such thing. He was quite popular with the people, apparently, but not with the Jewish leaders – I suppose they felt he was a threat to their authority. Anyway, that seemed to settle down without any need for us to interfere, but I believe that he came into the city several times through the week, and there were some angry scenes in the temple that got the tribune on edge.

Come the last day before the feast, we found out that the Jewish leaders had staged a midnight raid on the Mount of Olives to capture this popular leader. They held an all-night trial of their own and then did their best to convince the governor to execute him. I won't bore you with all the details, but the result was that early in the morning, Pilate called me to take this man to Herod Antipas on the basis that he was from somewhere in Herod's jurisdiction. I took the man – Jesus was his name – with a force of soldiers, and delivered him to Herod's soldiers. We stood by, waiting and watching. Herod came out to see him, and that was the first indication I had that this man was different from most of the criminals we have to deal with. It was obvious that Herod had been eager to see Jesus – who was apparently quite famous in Herod's area – yet the man would not answer his questions! I don't know, but it wouldn't surprise me if he could have escaped without any significant punishment if he had just cooperated with Herod.

Somehow, the chief priests and scribes had heard of our mission, and they arrived while Herod was speaking to him.

It didn't take long for Herod to get angry with him – probably aided by the presence of the chief priests – and his reactions were just what you would expect from one of the Herods. He began to treat the man with contempt and encouraged his soldiers to do the same – not that they needed much encouragement. Still the man did not respond.

Then he dressed the man in a fine garment and handed him back to me and my men. Herod came back with us to see Pilate, and the two of them disappeared into the governor's offices, suddenly seeming much friendlier than I have ever seen them before.

The next I heard of the whole business was when Pilate called me and told me to get Barabbas ready to be freed. Barabbas! The man was a petty thief who had also been involved in a rebellion, and yet the chief priests wanted <u>him</u> freed in preference to Jesus. What hypocrisy! They accused Jesus of inciting rebellion against Rome, and yet they wanted to free a man who had been involved in an actual rebellion against Rome! Those chief priests are good company for someone like Barabbas.

After a while, Pilate gathered the whole battalion together and encouraged us to scourge Jesus. Most of the soldiers were quite happy to get involved: trying to supervise the Jews is a frustrating task. It didn't stop with scourging either – they dressed him in another fancy robe and put a crown of thorns on him, then started hitting him on the head and mocking him, calling him "the King of the Jews."

Life isn't always fair or easy, and sometimes innocent people suffer because of pent-up frustrations. This man was an example.

Guarding the dying

He was beaten and mocked – treated very cruelly – and he responded with silence. He didn't complain, he didn't shout, he didn't try to justify himself. Just imagine what things would be like for you now if you'd never said anything when Mrs S was gossiping about you?

That got my attention, but it didn't make me admire him.

What did make me admire him was the way he behaved when we actually crucified him.

For a start, his lack of complaining continued, even though almost everybody seemed to be laughing at him. He was crucified between two criminals, and at the start, they were both sneering at him. So were the Jewish rulers, the chief priests, the scribes, the Pharisees and the elders, as well as many other people, including my men.

Then one of the criminals pointed out to the other one that they were getting what they deserved, but that Jesus, so he said, didn't deserve what he was getting. Then he asked Jesus to remember him when he came in his kingdom. All this honourableness was catching!

Another thing I admired was the way he showed his care for others despite his situation. It seems that his mother was there watching, and Jesus spoke to one of the men who was also watching and told him to look after her. I'm not sure that I could worry about you if I was being crucified, Mum!

There were also two strange phenomena while he was on the cross: first, it went dark for three hours before he died, and then when he did die, there was an earthquake. Did those things come because of this man? I'm not sure, but I think they probably did. I've never seen a man behaving like that on a cross, and I'm sure he was a righteous man, not a criminal. That's what the criminal said, and I'm agreeing with a criminal.

Well, he's dead now, and so is the criminal who praised him. All the leaders who mocked him are still alive, but the day after he died, they were so worried that he might come back to life again that they asked Pilate to put a guard on the tomb. Imagine that – a guard on the tomb of a dead man!

It all adds up to too much for me. This was the strangest crucifixion I have ever attended, and the strangest man I have ever crucified. At the end of it all, I am convinced that he is a better man than all of the people who were killing him, and with that strange darkness and the earthquake, I can't help wondering whether he could have done more to escape if he had chosen to do so.

Anyway, I think that I might try to find out more about this man. After all, there are rumours floating around that he rose from the dead three days after we killed him. Some people are even claiming that they meet him daily.

What do you reckon, Mum?

Have I gone mad, worrying about a dead man?

Lots of love,

Your dutiful son,

Lucius

So that's how it was. A very strange series of events surrounding the strange execution of a very unusual man who showed no signs of being a criminal. Since then, I've been able to find out a bit more information, but it's not easy.

I've got in touch with a few of his followers, but they're all very suspicious of a centurion who is asking questions about Jesus.

Anyway, maybe it's only important for Jews, but I can't help thinking that when he said, "Father, forgive them for they don't know what they are doing," it seemed to be aimed most at us Romans who were crucifying him. I wouldn't mind some forgiveness for that particular job – I really didn't know what I was doing.

Twenty

The Tale of Tabitha

by Laura Morgan

For the true story, read Acts 9:36-42.

Tabitha was always so helpful to us — to everybody, in fact.

For years I watched her helping everyone else and admired what she did, but back then it never occurred to me that one day I might need her help myself. With a houseful of children, I was certainly kept busy, but with my husband in regular work as a labourer, we were getting on quite well.

We were both staunch believers in The Way and enjoyed our fellowship with the other believers in Joppa, including Tabitha and her husband.

But working as a labourer has its dangers, and one day, about a year after we were baptised into Jesus' name, the worst happened. I was returning from the market with our two youngest children when I was met by a running figure that I recognised as one of the men who worked with my husband.

"Your husband's had an accident," he shouted, "a block fell on him!"

I wished the children were not there to hear the terrible news, although they would have had to know later. For a moment I was numb with shock. Somehow I had always assumed that he would be kept safe despite the accidents that were all too common.

"Is he badly hurt?" I asked sharply.

"It looks," said the man between gasps, "as if he'll be out of work for quite a while."

"But he'll live?" I could not help asking, seeing the expression on his face.

He wouldn't look at me. "How would I know?" Such was my fear that it scarcely registered that the man was muttering prayers.

I was praying desperately to the one God who could actually help — the God of The Way.

As I hurried to see my husband, who had by that time been carried home, I was still praying, yet more urgently as I saw the pain in his face. He tried to smile, but it was not convincing; he was obviously badly injured.

The next couple of days passed in a blur. The only thing I remembered later was Tabitha, helpful, kind Tabitha, appearing on my doorstep and asking what she could do for me.

She was always helping the poor, and with a jolt, I realised that, without a regular income, that would soon be us.

As I nursed my husband, she managed everything that I couldn't: our clothing, our food, and even the children when the pain of my husband's broken body was too great for him to bear and I could not leave his side. I did what I could, but my husband never recovered from that accident. He died with his faith and a hope for the future, but I was left a widow, our children fatherless.

Through it all Tabitha helped me.

I thought I had been busy before my husband died, but after that I realised what being busy really meant, as I took on suitable work to take some of the financial burden off the other believers. Without Tabitha's help, though, we could not have coped. She made all our clothes — and let me tell you, active, healthy children go through clothes at a fair rate! — without ever being asked, and not only ours. Countless others benefited from her skill and willingness to help — and she never wanted thanks, either, except where it could be directed towards God for giving her such skills and the time to use them. I followed her advice and thanked God.

I do not how long she had been ceaselessly doing good for everyone, yet never neglecting her husband. All I knew was that she was growing old. To work was her choice, however, and we let her continue — not that we could have stopped her — though she was perhaps slowing down.

But then, a few days ago, Tabitha suddenly became ill — badly ill. The first intimation I had of it was the sight of her husband running towards me as I left the house to go to the well for water. The situation was so similar to when I heard that my husband had been hurt that I knew, somehow, what he was going to say.

"It's Tabitha," he said, and fear strained his voice. "She's lying on the floor and I can't rouse her."

"Should I tell others?" I asked quickly. Of the believers, our house was closest to theirs, so it made sense he would come to me first. I guessed that he probably wanted to return to her. "One of us can call the doctor, and I can get the other believers to pray."

"Please do."

I asked our neighbour to go and get the doctor, and then hurried around to the homes of the other believers. When I went, at last, to Tabitha, I could tell immediately that she was badly ill; only by a miracle could she survive this mysterious illness. But miracles do happen through the Holy Spirit, so we did not lose hope. We spent all of that day keeping her as comfortable as we could and praying for her recovery, but she kept on getting worse.

That evening, she died. The miracle we had hoped and prayed for had not come. If only one of the apostles had been in Joppa, she could have been made healthy again.

All we could do for her was done; we washed her body and placed it in an upper room. Normally, of course, we would have buried her immediately, but one of the brothers who had come to the house after finishing his work for the day happened to mention that Peter was in Lydda, only sixteen kilometres[24] away. I can't remember who suggested asking Peter to come from Lydda. We were all still praying for a miracle — though we weren't clear as to what — desperate to show how much we appreciated her, and more, how much we loved her. Early the next morning, therefore, the leaders sent two men to see if Peter could come. Their words must have been convincingly urgent, because he arrived in Joppa that afternoon.

---

[24] 10 miles.

We were all gathered at the house when he arrived, still praying, refusing to completely give up hope; yet by that time we scarcely had any hope left. She was dead....

None of the weeping widows there — myself included — could bear to sit in complete idleness, so we each brought various garments Tabitha had made for us and sat reminiscing about her. We wanted to remember how hard she had worked to serve others, and to show Peter, too. Whenever we managed to control our sobbing for a time, it wasn't long before it would begin once more, our grief fuelled by that of everyone else.

She had been so kind to all of us.

Peter glanced around at us. I said shakily, "She — she made these garments for us."

"Yes!" wept another. "She made them all, everything we needed!"

"Such an inspiration!" added an older widow, tears flowing freely down her worn face.

Peter listened, then watched us, and said at last, plainly upset by our sorrow, "Please go out of the room, all of you."

We left, although I wondered why he wanted us to leave. What was happening?

We did not have to wonder for long.

A short time later, Peter stepped out of the room, glanced around at the group of us and said with a smile, "Please come back in."

Slightly puzzled, we entered the room, her husband near the front of the group. What...?

Tabitha was standing up, smiling — alive.

"What happened? She's alive!" her husband cried, a look of delight flooding his grief-stricken face. The rest of us reacted with varying degrees of amazement — but all with joy and thankfulness.

Tabitha herself was looking a little disoriented, and turned to look questioningly at Peter, obviously wondering why we were all reacting this way.

"I prayed," said Peter simply, "and told her to get up. She opened her eyes and sat up, so I helped her up and told her to wait until you all came in. That was all."

"Wait," said Tabitha, looking confused. "What was wrong with me?"

"You were ill," I answered, "and then you... died." I swallowed and continued, "But now Peter has come and you're alive again."

"And I feel... younger, too," Tabitha said slowly. She looked wonderingly at Peter. "Praise the Lord! If — if anyone needs anything I can do...." She did not have to finish her sentence.

"Praise the Lord," I repeated even as I smiled at her words, and I wasn't the only one. It was such a typical Tabitha reaction. That she was well again delighted me, not from any sense of personal gain but because I wanted her to be well. And she clearly was. She looked younger, stronger, happier.

She had been dead, and now she was alive again. Our tears of grief, not yet dry, became tears of joy.

Tabitha was an encouragement to all of us. Now God had truly blessed her by resurrecting her, making it clear that he approved of what she was doing. I found myself wishing to emulate her, for once not even thinking of the extra work it would entail since I had a fairly large family of my own. She was such an example of how we could be like Jesus in serving others. Now we needed to share it with the world.

And Tabitha could work beside us!

Twenty-One

Outrage!

For the true story, see Acts 15:1-35 and Galatians 2:11-14.

Let me start by getting this straight: I am a follower of Jesus. Not a boss, an overlord, a dictator or an autocrat – unlike others whom I could name.

However, by God's grace, I do hold a position of leadership amongst the believers and have often been able to help others through my understanding of scripture. I have studied the Law of Moses for many years and can see in it many links to Jesus as our saviour. I have also, for many years, been a Pharisee.

Unfortunately, though, many amongst the believers are now calling the Law the "old covenant", as if there is nothing we can learn from it.

Worse, some of the less educated brothers amongst us have seized on this terminology and ignorantly claim that we should abandon Moses' Law altogether. They say that we should ignore the laws, the feasts and even – would you believe it? – circumcision.

Yet even that is not the worst of it. Worse even than those who don't know better are some who should know better, but still do their best to coerce others into discarding the laws that God gave to Israel.

Jesus himself said: "I did not come to abolish the law." Since Jesus did not come to abolish the law, why are some believers trying to do so?

Jesus encouraged us to be servants and to practice humility, so I do not try to insist that everybody follow me and acknowledge me as a great leader; unfortunately, however, it seems that various others do want to make such demands for themselves. Even people who came very late to a belief in Jesus seem to feel that they have a right to override everybody else and enforce their opinions on the majority! Some also have a way of convincing others to follow their ideas, and are not shy about using those powers.

It is fair to say that I am outraged and disgusted – but I am also very concerned about the future of The Way. I joined the fellowship because I believed that Jesus was the Messiah promised to our people, the prophet Moses had spoken about, the son of David. It was clear that there had to be some changes to our way of life to follow Jesus, but now I am concerned that we are going too far; throwing out the grain along with the chaff!

I can't keep quiet about this because I fear that if things continue the way they're going, The Way will just become another of the many cults that have come and gone over the years. Yet we have truth, if only we can maintain it.

So, now I want to explain what has made me so upset.

In Jerusalem and other parts of Judea there are many Pharisees like me who have believed in Jesus. Jesus' preaching forced us to review our religion, and when we did so, we had to admit that he was right when he called us "hypocrites" not long before he was crucified.

We opened our minds and softened our hearts, then swallowed our pride and welcomed Jesus as our saviour.

We told our friends about him, and did our best to spread the hope of salvation to all we met. We taught people about how Jesus was the fulfilment of the promises made in the Law and the prophets. We encouraged people to continue to follow the Law just as Jesus had done. After all, Jesus attended the synagogue every Sabbath, and so many of his teachings came directly from the Law. His answers to temptation, to his enemies' questions and to those who genuinely wanted to learn the truth of God all included reference to Scripture. Indeed, one of his criticisms of his enemies was that they did not know the Scriptures – and he was referring to our Hebrew Scriptures. Those writings also speak of his coming, so it all makes a very clear picture.

But apparently not to some. Some treat the law as outdated, outmoded, superseded and useless. Imagine that! The Law that guided David and the prophets, provided Jesus' most compelling arguments, showcases the holiness of God and shows his love for Israel – being discarded!

A few months ago, some of my friends, fellow believers, started to hear some disturbing stories from Antioch in Syria, where a congregation had formed years ago soon after Stephen was martyred and we had to run for our lives. Initially it was made up entirely of Jews, then some believers from Cyprus and Cyrene began to speak to Greeks. I suppose that wasn't all bad; most of those Greeks had a passing knowledge of Judaism, and they were quickly convinced about Jesus and his resurrection. However, things were moving too swiftly and it sounded like it was becoming a free-for-all. When the leaders in Jerusalem heard about it, they sent Barnabas to see what was going on. To be honest, I was a bit disappointed with Barnabas – he was there only a short time before giving it all his blessing and moving on. It would have been better if he had stayed and kept a guiding hand on the tiller.

Instead, he seems to have gone to Tarsus specifically to find Saul, an unexpected convert who had been a Pharisee like me – but one who was very much on the side of the chief priests in the beginning, including standing with them when Stephen was murdered.

We had all been very suspicious of him when we heard that he had been converted, but he seemed genuine, and deeply humbled by the experience of seeing a living Jesus. For several years he kept very quiet, but anyone who has worked for and lost a position of importance in the past is likely to try again sometime.

Anyway, Barnabas returned to Antioch with Saul, and together they did seem to help to settle things down for a time. Then after a year or so, they went on a journey together through Cyprus, Pamphylia and other places, preaching The Way. I suppose it should have been predictable that working among Gentiles for years would affect even people with strict backgrounds like Barnabas and Saul. Whatever the reason, by the time Saul returned he seemed changed. He had even changed his name and wanted everyone to call him Paul.

Presumably while they were away, their ideas slowly changed and became more lax. Standards are always hard to maintain, and if you mix too much with people who have no idea of God's laws then your morals are likely to suffer. Not only that, but being admired and praised all the time can go to your head. Through the power of the Holy Spirit, Saul was able to perform many miracles, and I guess it must be hard to keep your balance when you can do that.

I don't want to be critical, of course, but when I met him some time after that journey, he seemed less humble, and more eager to be a leader among the believers.

Anyway, some friends and I went to Antioch because of those concerning reports. Peter had been there for a while, so you might think that there wouldn't be any need to worry, with one of the apostles there, but Peter... well, he's Peter, and it was clear that the situation wasn't great.

When we arrived, he welcomed us and we discussed the wonderful way in which God was calling the Gentiles to join us in the faith. He had some Gentiles with him at the time, but we suggested tactfully that we had some private business to discuss – matters for true Israelites only – and Peter sent them away. That let us get down to business: how the Gentiles needed to take on the Law. Peter's response to the question of how many Gentile converts had been circumcised was a bit evasive, so we reminded him of the need for circumcision so that we could welcome Gentile believers as sons of Abraham.

Everything was going well until it came to mealtime. Peter, naturally, ate separately with us, since we Jews all know the requirements for cleanliness and holiness. We were having a relaxed meal, us in one corner of the room and the Gentile believers across the other side, when in stormed Paul. His eyes were positively flashing with anger and he immediately marched across to Peter, who was sitting right next to me, and began berating him! No private communication, no "Can I talk to you quietly," or anything like that – just straight into it in front of everyone. Well, you can imagine just how shocked I was. This former persecutor criticising one of the Master's 12 disciples in public!

He accused Peter of having behaved like a Gentile until we came and then trying to insist that Gentiles should behave like Jews.

It was terribly embarrassing. I did my best to defend Peter and to make a stand for the Law of God, but Paul's manner was overbearing and opinionated....

℞

I wrote that stinging assessment of events several months ago, the night after it all blew up.

Last week, I took it out and read it over. With all that has happened since, I almost burned it straight away. Instead, I decided to show it to a friend so that we could discuss together what the outcome had been. (There were a few more sentences at the end; I did burn those – I should never have written them, and the anger I felt at the time is no excuse.) We talked about it for hours and felt that we learned some serious lessons. However, I don't want my diatribe to survive, because it is a worrying example of how far wrong honest people can go without realising it.

Let me explain.

The discussions that day were very heated, and at the time I felt that I and my friends were completely in the right. We had been followers of Jesus for more than 15 years. We had confidence in our faith and confidence that we understood the truth that Jesus had taught. Yet we were wrong.

Shortly afterwards, a conference was arranged in Jerusalem where the apostles and elders met together to discuss whether the Gentiles had to follow the Law of Moses or not.

I arrived at the conference with a certainty that God would help truth to prevail, and an equal certainty of what that truth was! I wanted – and expected – an unequivocal statement that the Gentiles must follow Moses' Law.

Yet as the discussion progressed, it became clear that the work of Paul and Barnabas in foreign lands had been blessed by God. God had been calling Gentiles to his way without demanding that they turn into Jews.

Peter reminded the audience that God had shown through him that the Gentiles could be saved through faith just as we Jews could be. He made no attempt to criticise Paul or reject what he had said in Antioch; instead, he agreed with Paul that there was no distinction between Jews and Gentiles.

Likewise, Paul made no attempt to ridicule Peter or to look for arguments; instead, the two of them worked together to achieve unity and convince doubters like me that this was God's will.

And with God's blessing, it worked! What giants of faith they are!

These words make it sound as if I found it easy to change my views, but I most certainly did not. More than 15 years of belief cannot be overturned in just a few moments. But the experience did teach me humility. Both Peter and Paul showed it, and I have tried to learn it too, because if we want unity, we need to have humility first.

I also learned a really important lesson: how long I had believed in Jesus didn't matter. What mattered was whether I was willing to soften my heart and really listen to what he taught. Teaching us Jews first was part of God's faithfulness to Abraham, but so was calling the Gentiles so that all nations could truly be blessed in Abraham.

I hope that my heart has finally opened up to God's teaching, and I'm trying hard to read our Scriptures with an open mind and learn.

How much I have learned over the last few months – I who really thought that I already understood it all!

Twenty-Two

One Wet Night

For the true story, see Acts 27:13-28:10.

I'm really going to have to think about what all of this means. Just a few weeks ago, I was quite satisfied with my religion: I felt at ease with how I worshipped the gods and was comfortable enough with what it all meant – but it's been a strange few weeks.

As it does each year, winter has come to Melita, and with it the terrible storms that take so many lives at sea. Nothing unusual about that. The boats people sail on seem so big and safe when the sea is calm, but they don't do so well when the nor'easter starts blowing. When all is said and done, they're just cockleshells. When the wind whips up the waves and black clouds go scudding across the sea for weeks on end, the place to be is on land, in a nice dry house.

You would think that people would learn that winter storms are best watched from land. Surely it's better to wait until spring than to take the risk? But instead, every year people try to push the envelope, cut things fine, walk the tightrope and go to extremes, travelling too late in the year. Later than is safe.

And it often ends in disaster.

Then we pick up the pieces. Literally. When really bad storms lash the area, all sorts of things wash up on the shore, from storage containers to pieces of masts or even empty boats. Many of us comb the beaches after big storms in search of any items that we can use, or that can earn us money.

The Romans like to call the sea "Our Sea", because they govern all of the land around the coast, but the number of shipwrecks that occur every year should make it very clear that they don't control the sea!

Anyway, recently there was a big storm that continued for about two weeks. It was good to watch from the shore – I have always revelled in the raw power of the massive waves as they roll across the bay and climb the beach or crash against the cliffs that flank it.

One day as it was starting to ease a little, I went down to the shore in the early morning. It was crazy going out into such weather: the wind was still gale force, and the cold rain cut into my face as I leaned into the wind, making my way along the track that skirts the bay. Often at that time of morning there would be many on the road, bringing back their catches from the sea, but on that wild morning I was alone on the road as I crested the rise and looked down on the surging grey waters. Daylight was coming slowly and the monstrous waves were climbing high up the beach, striving to reach the boats that had been dragged up almost onto the track.

The noise of wind and wave was thunderous and the grand beauty of the scene tugged at my heart as it always does.

Storms are lovely to look at from dry land, but I never go out to sea. The maelstrom that covers the reef near the middle of the bay claimed the life of a dear uncle some years ago, and I am content to admire the pitiless, writhing water from a safe distance.

I quickly scanned the beach for any obvious flotsam but there was none, so I crouched on a sand hill in the biting rain and watched the storm. Visibility was poor and I could only catch occasional glimpses of the entrance to the bay where the surging waters were even wilder.

Crouching down protected me little from the elements but though I enjoyed watching the majestic progress of the storm, I was gradually getting colder. It was well beyond time to go – my hands felt as if they were frozen solid – when the rain eased for a few moments and the wind seemed to pause to take a breath. Briefly, in the distance, just beyond where the headlands curved together and almost met, I saw a shadowy, grey shape.

In the few moments before the wind resumed its full force, I made out the shape of a large ship, rolling sluggishly in the surging waves; then once more the wind whipped up the spray and reduced visibility almost to nothing.

When people see something they don't expect, they sometimes say that they can't believe their eyes, but I have never felt like that. I *saw* that ship, and I knew immediately that a disaster was unfolding out there, beyond the headlands.

I had to get help.

There are a few huts near the beach and I know the people there a little, so I ran quickly to the closest one.

"There's a shipwreck coming," I said, banging on the door and shouting to make myself heard over the keening of the wind.

It was only a few moments before the man of the house opened the door, wrapping a heavy coat around himself as he stepped out into the icy rain to meet me.

"What do you mean?" he asked. "Where?"

"Out there, just outside the bay," I bellowed, pointing. "Tell the others who live around here. I'm going up to the town to get more helpers. It looks like a big ship, and it'll never land safely – not with the reef there."

Thankfully, he was willing to trust me, despite the appalling conditions which completely hid the ship from sight. I left in a hurry and ran along the track, over the rise and down into the town. The wind was less fierce in the hollow, but it was still not the day for a summer picnic.

I'm related to most of the people in the town, so I planned to knock on the doors of some of the best seafarers and the biggest, strongest men we have. As an afterthought, I also included Thanatos, my cousin: he is an undertaker.

By the time I had told the few details I knew about 20 times, I had worked out the wording pretty well. It didn't take long to tell all that I knew in a convincing and urgent manner. I was already worried about what I would find when I made my way back to the beach, so I didn't bother with the last few names on my mental list. Last of all, though, I did go to my cousin – I was sure he would be needed.

Thanatos and I made our way to the beach, and it was immediately clear that I had been right to be worried. The rain had stopped and the ship was now in plain sight. With her foresail bellied out in the wind, she was making her way swiftly across the bay, making for the beach. Anyone who knew the bay would have warned the pilot about the reef, and men on the beach were trying to do so, but it was too late.

There was no sudden shock or loud noise, the ship just stopped. One moment it was cutting smoothly through the heaving waters, running eagerly ahead of them towards the safety of the beach, and the next the bow seemed to shiver a little and many of the figures crowded on the deck stumbled and fell as the ship came to a sudden stop, the bow immovably caught on that terrible reef.

Within moments, the water was seething around the ship as it lay stationary and the waves rushed past it towards the shore. The wind was still blowing in my face, and I shivered with cold and fear as the ship was repeatedly lifted up by the waves, only to crash down onto the reef again as each wave passed. No sound reached us above the roar of the wind and the waves, but I was sure that the planks of the ship must be taking a terrible pounding. It wouldn't be long before the ship broke up.

How many would die in this disaster? A ship that size could have hundreds on board and we would be powerless to help them.

Ships are much tougher than people; in the end it was about five hours before the ship finally broke up. As the end approached, we began to see people jumping into the sea. Obviously they could all swim and we saw bobbing heads miraculously swimming towards us. I don't think I could have stayed afloat in that seething mass of water, but gradually we saw more and more people standing up in the shallows and making their way up the beach. I was amazed by the numbers successfully reaching safety.

"It's amazing how many people are escaping from the wreck," I said to Thanatos.

"Yes," he said, dourly, "but just wait until we get to the ones who can't swim. It'll be a catastrophe."

I thought that he was probably right, but when the ship finally started breaking apart, everyone left aboard seemed to be able to grab a plank or something else that would float. Holding on tightly, they jumped or fell into the raging sea, and I was sure that we were watching an utter disaster unfolding.

But I was wrong.

For the next few minutes, we saw plenty of heads bobbing about in the waves, arms clinging desperately to whatever was keeping them afloat. No-one dared to take a boat out into that storm to help anyone – it would merely have meant the deaths of more helpless victims.

Amazingly enough, though, after a while, some of the planks and bobbing heads began to reach the shore, then more and more, until eventually there were crowds of bedraggled, shivering refugees being welcomed to Melita.

Some of the first to arrive were Roman soldiers who were able to swim, but they weren't the imperious, overbearing soldiers that we often see on Melita. Instead, they were unarmed and unarmored fugitives from the waves, their red tunics alone making it clear that they were soldiers. They huddled and shivered like the rest of the passengers. Before long, they had told us that some of the ship's cargo – yes, that's what they called them, "cargo" – were criminals who were being transported to Rome. That didn't make us feel any too happy, but still, we had to do what we could to help them all.

We couldn't make an exact count immediately, but I was sure that there were well over a hundred people on the beach, and more were still coming.

Thanatos seemed almost a little disappointed by the amazing number of people who were escaping from the sea, but I have to admit he came up with a good idea then.

"Why don't we light a fire?" he asked. "You know, dry these people out. Warm them up."

"Good idea," I agreed, and began collecting some wood. After a while, we recruited some others to help, while I went to my home to get some dry wood and kindling. I could see that we weren't going to get the fire started otherwise. As I was returning, the rain resumed, so it wasn't easy to get the fire going. A few of the locals also brought some dry wood, and some of the passengers from the ship began collecting sticks to help too.

One of these was a man called Paul. He was a prisoner being taken to Rome and I didn't know what he had done wrong – but he seemed a nice enough sort of man and he was certainly quick to help us feed the fire. He didn't stop when the fire was burning warmly either, but kept bringing more despite the freezing rain. Then, as he threw one of his bundles of sticks on the blazing fire, a viper came out of the bundle and bit him.

Now, these vipers can be deadly – although it depends on how much of a grip they get on their victim. Well, this one got a good grip, I can tell you! There Paul stood with the snake dangling from his hand, and when the men standing near him saw it, they began to shout and quickly stepped back, away from the creature.

I have to say that Paul was remarkably casual about it. Too casual, I thought. He gave the impression that he didn't care, and that's not normal. For a few moments he just stood there, the snake on his hand wriggling around frantically, trying to escape from the heat. Then Paul just shook the beast off and it fell into the hottest part of the fire, where it could be seen writhing and squirming for a little while, although it was already beginning to turn black from the heat.

Thanatos has a dry sort of voice; it always sounds serious and becomes rather dismal when unpleasant things happen. We had both been standing near Paul when the serpent struck, although we were considerably further away by the time he said in his dullest voice, "He must be a murderer, don't you see? He escaped from the sea, but Justice won't let him live."

He was expressing one of the things that a few of us had been worried about: who wanted to have criminals – maybe thugs and murderers – on our peaceful island?

Even so, it was sad to see someone who had been so helpful get bitten by one of those killer snakes. I tried to get Paul to sit down and rest, since that seems to help sometimes with snakebites, but he wouldn't have any of it. He just looked at me and smiled, then went back to collecting more sticks for the fire! Thanatos and I watched him carefully, wondering how long he would last before the snake poison got him....

Justice is important, I think, and I had always felt that it seemed to work like a principle in the world. Quite simply, good and just people had good things happen to them, whereas evil people were punished, often by things that seemed like chance occurrences. When a rock or a large tree fell on someone, it wasn't hard to see things that they had done that could have triggered such a judgement.

We didn't know enough about this Paul to know his exact crime, but we did know that he was being taken to Rome as a prisoner, so he must have had something to hide. Now justice had caught up with him.

So we waited.

Normally these vipers cause suffering pretty quickly, so we all expected his confident smile to desert him very soon, and for him to stop collecting sticks too; but no, he just kept going and didn't even have the bite treated. Even if the viper was not venomous, surely its fangs would have left some painful puncture wounds? Maybe so, but Paul kept on picking up sticks and we kept watching.

And waiting.

You know what it's like when you are confidently waiting for something and slowly begin to realise that there must be something wrong with your assumptions?

Thanatos and I kept looking at each other, and I couldn't help pursing my lips and frowning as I began to see that somewhere our conclusions must have gone awry. Paul wasn't swelling up. He wasn't falling down dead. He wasn't even in pain. He was happy and healthy, and above all, eager to tell us all just how thankful he was to his God that everyone had been saved from the shipwreck!

This time, I was the one who finally announced the obvious solution to the conundrum: "If a snake can't even hurt him, he must be a god."

"Maybe you're right," mused Thanatos, and I have to admit that his voice sounded more animated than normal. "He must be the one who saved everyone in the ship. There's no way they could all have escaped alive from that wreck without something supernatural happening. I was certain that I would have lots of corpses to look after. You're right, he must be a god!"

We discussed among ourselves how wonderful it was to have a god visiting us and even began to feel rather proud of ourselves – gaining importance by association. We talked about how we could honour him, and I hoped inwardly that he wouldn't remember our earlier suggestion that he must be a murderer.

After a while, Paul noticed our whispering and our admiring glances and asked what we were chattering about. When I think back on it, he really did seem rather down-to-earth – not god-like at all. And then his response was nothing like what I expected: "Are you crazy?" he asked – he even looked a little angry. "Haven't you listened to anything I've been saying about why we were saved from the sea? It wasn't me – I'm just a man like you. It was the God who made the world. He wants to lead you away from all of these gods that you imagine are working in the world. He saved everyone on board our ship, and saved me again when the snake bit me. Worship him, but whatever you do, don't worship me! God has put up with this sort of ignorance for long enough, and now he wants everyone, everywhere, to worship him as the only true God."

Paul continued talking for quite a while, explaining his beliefs and his hope for the future. I acknowledged to myself that it was hard to argue with him, given his miraculous survival despite both shipwreck and snakebite, but I still wasn't really convinced that it mattered much – not until a few days later.

That was when Paul cured the father of Publius, the chief man of Melita. Publius had taken over the care of the whole ship's company – the sort of generous hospitality that we of Melita like to think we are famous for, and for which we're proud of our leaders when they show it so clearly. At that particular time, Publius was terribly worried about his father, who was very sick and not really expected to live. Nevertheless, hospitality must come first.

Paul was touched by this attitude and asked if he could visit the dying man. Publius tried to dissuade him, but Paul was apparently quite insistent that he should do so. I wasn't surprised when I heard that; Paul had struck me as a very forceful personality, though in a kind way – if you know what I mean.

I would've dearly loved to have been there and seen what happened, but apparently it was as simple as Paul walking into the room, then praying and putting his hands on the man. That's all it took to heal Publius' father. He sat up in bed, feeling a little tired, but pleased that the terrible pain and fever had suddenly gone. Within a day he was up and about – and feeling better than he had done for years, he said.

That was the third piece of evidence that Paul was something special, so I knew I couldn't ignore it – that would have been foolish. I was determined to find out about him and his religion. So I went to where he was staying and spoke to the doctor who was travelling with him. The doctor's name was Luke, and he tried to explain to me exactly what had been wrong with Publius' father. That was a waste of time, because I couldn't understand the technical details. Nevertheless, I did find it easy to understand when he went on to tell me that Paul had cured hundreds, maybe even thousands of sick people.

"So he *is* a god?" I asked, impressed.

Luke gave a pained smile. "No, he is not a god," he said. "If I had a sestertius for every time someone has suggested that he is a god or a demi-god I would be a very rich man! But no. Paul is just a man like you and me."

"Then how does he do these miracles? How come snakes can't even hurt him?"

"It is the God he worships who does the miracles," said Luke.

"But the gods don't like helping mere mortals, do they? They don't want us doing miracles! Very protective of their powers, people tell me."

"The gods you are referring to are not gods at all. In fact, there is only one God, who made the world and everything in it."

"One god? Only one?"

"Yes. Why do you think there is more than one?"

"Well, that's what everyone says, isn't it? How would I know anyway? I've sometimes wondered if we need any at all," I said.

"Ah," said Luke, "Now you're starting to think! That's good, but if there is no God, how come we are alive? Where did we come from? Who made the world? Who made us? It can't all just happen from nothing, can it?"

"No, I suppose it takes something to do something."

"Yes, it does. We can see that fact around us all the time – in a simple way. A lump of rock does nothing by itself, but a living thing can do something. So where did life come from?"

"That was the cosmic egg, wasn't it?"

"If so, who made the egg?"

"Well, yes, I suppose that something must have made it, so that doesn't really help, does it?"

"Have you heard of the God of the Jews?"

"No."

"You need to know some history, but he is the God who made the world, sent the flood, chose Israel as his nation, took them out of Egypt and gave them the land of Israel," said Luke. "He is the only God, and that's the only explanation of the universe that really makes sense. And, of course, I have seen people who believe in that one God do amazing miracles – impossible things – which they say come from him. To me, it all adds up to a rather convincing picture. That's why I believe in the same God as Paul does. You've seen some of these miracles too, so they should have opened your mind to thinking seriously about this God. He is Lord of heaven and earth; the creator who made us and all living things, and put the nations where he wanted them."[25]

---

[25] Most of the arguments attributed to Luke here are taken from Paul's words in Acts 17:24-31 when speaking to the people at the Areopagus, with a thought from 1 John 4:14 as well.

"But does it matter if I believe that? I mean – so what if he's the creator?"

Luke looked at me and said, "I suppose that the main thing is that if he has the power to create us and we are his offspring, then it's not up to us to decide how we should worship him. We shouldn't think that he is like gold or silver or stone, an image formed by the art and imagination of man." Luke paused, and his expression was searching. He clearly wanted to determine my response to his words, but I wasn't sure of it myself. His argument seemed reasonable: after all, if there was a creator who made us all, it made sense that he might want to tell us how to worship him, rather than us doing whatever we want.

"That makes some sense," I said cautiously, and Luke seemed satisfied enough with my response.

"God has overlooked such ignorance about worship in the past," he continued, "but now he commands all people everywhere to repent, because he has fixed a day when he will judge the world in righteousness by a man whom he has appointed."

That seemed a little strange to me and I must have shown my puzzlement, because Luke stopped.

"What's wrong with that?" he asked.

"Well, if he is the only God as you say, and he wants to judge the world, why would he do it through a man?"

"That's a really good question," said Luke, and he seemed to mean it. I'm not used to being complimented on the quality of my religious questions – I was so surprised that I almost missed what he said next.

"You see, God sent his son to be the saviour of the world, but he is also to be the judge; and God has given proof of this to everyone by raising him from the dead."

As you might imagine, that answer raised even more questions, and Luke and I ended up talking about religion for hours. Me! – A man who appreciates the basic ideas of right and wrong, but who has always been too busy with the everyday things of life to think much about religion. I've always left the nitty-gritty of worship to priests and oracles and done what I was told.

But what Luke said made sense.

I liked the idea of one God who had made everything. Creation has a beauty and a grandeur that thrills me, but it also has a terrifying power that is beyond the ability of humans to tame. Yet Paul and Luke and all the others on the doomed ship had been saved through a storm that had made even expert seamen give up hope. A God who can first create such storms and then tame them to save his servants also fitted with the ideas of judgement and salvation, but I had to find out more.

As Luke and I talked on into the evening, Paul returned. Apparently he had been talking to Publius, and he seemed full of the same sort of excitement that I had seen in Luke as he tried to explain to me all about God and his son, Jesus. It was a joyous excitement that seemed infectious. I have never met people who can make religion seem more sensible and just completely... normal. They don't seem to think of religion as a special compartment in their life. Maybe it's because they have dedicated their life to working as missionaries. Whatever the reason, they have given me a lot to think about and many questions to answer.

It started with a catastrophic shipwreck that didn't turn out to be catastrophic at all, and then my deeper interest was triggered by the events of that stormy day when Paul picked up a bundle of sticks and was bitten by a snake.

I'm sure that snake didn't know that its bite would help Paul to preach about the God who made them both!

About the authors

Mark Morgan was born in Australia during 1963; the youngest son of Peter and Meryl Morgan. Deeply involved in religion all of his life, he has worked as a lay preacher, Sunday School teacher and missionary – trying to balance the many demands of spiritual life with those of family and paid employment.

After graduating, he worked in engineering for several years before concentrating on software development. Happily married and blessed with eight children, he has spent many years reading the Bible and learning to teach its lessons.

Writing Bible-based novels now fills much of his time.

Cathy Morgan considers herself to have been blessed to have parents who ensured that the entire family read the Bible together daily and did their best to make its stories and lessons interesting and memorable to a range of age groups, Cathy has been inspired by her Dad's work to branch out into occasional writing herself amidst a hotchpotch of employment, church, family and other commitments. In her free time, she's likely to be either reading or exploring the Grampians National Park, probably hunting for wildflowers.

Laura Morgan is the youngest daughter of Ruth and Mark Morgan and delights in reading the Bible and writing Bible-based fiction. School provides opportunities for writing, but also keeps her away from the writing she would prefer to do. Laura loves nature and revels in the beauty of sunsets, seeing God's hand around her in all things.

Free Download

Paul in Snippets

A 109-page PDF novelette by Mark Morgan.

The life of Paul painted from the Acts of the Apostles.

Get your free copy of *Paul in Snippets* when you sign up for the Bible Tales mailing list. As well as the eBook, you will receive a weekly email newsletter with micro tales, informative articles and special offers.

Visit **https://www.BibleTales.online/free-pins**

Bible Tales Online

Other books by Mark Morgan are available from Bible Tales Online.

Terror on Every Side!
THE LIFE OF JEREMIAH

From a family of priests in the peaceful reign of good King Josiah, came a young man Jeremiah, bringing words from God to his people. It was no message for the fainthearted, either. It was a message of *Terror on Every Side!*

Volume 1 – Early Days
Volume 2 – As Good As It Gets
Volume 3 – Darkness Falling
Volume 4 – The Darkness Deepens
Volume 5 – No Remedy

Generally available in hardcover, paperback, eBook and audiobook.

Micro-tales

Collections of short stories about Bible characters or events, available in paperback, eBook and audiobook.

Fiction Favours the Facts
Fiction Favours the Facts – Book 2

Other novels

Joseph, Rachel's son

Bible Tales Online continues to publish books.
To find the list of currently available books, visit

https://www.BibleTales.online/books

www.BibleTales.online

9 781925 587241